Penguin Books
People in Glass Houses

Shirley Hazzard was born and educated in Sydney, Australia. She has lived in the Far East, New Zealand, Italy and the United States. For ten years she worked for the United Nations Secretariat, resigning in 1962 to devote all her time to her writing. Many of her short stories have appeared in the *New Yorker* magazine, and a first collection of them, *Cliffs of Fall*, was published in 1963. Her first novel, *The Evening of the Holiday,* appeared in 1966, and has been published in a Penguin edition. A new novel, *The Bay of Noon*, will be published in 1970. Miss Hazzard and her husband, the writer Francis Steegmuller, live in New York.

Shirley Hazzard

People in Glass Houses

Penguin Books

Penguin Books Ltd, Harmondsworth,
Middlesex, England
Penguin Books Australia Ltd, Ringwood,
Victoria, Australia

First published by Macmillan 1967
Published in Penguin Books 1970

The contents of this book appeared in
slightly different form, in *The New Yorker*

Made and printed in Great Britain by
C. Nicholls & Company Ltd
Set in Linotype Granjon

For William Maxwell and Alan Maclean,
and in memory of Blanche W. Knopf

Contents

. . . and in such cases
Men's natures wrangle with inferior things,
Though great ones are their object.

OTHELLO, *Act* III, *Scene* IV

1. Nothing in Excess

'The aim of the Organization,' Mr Bekkus dictated, leaning back in his chair and casting up his eyes to the perforations of the sound-proof ceiling; 'The *aim* of the Organization,' he repeated with emphasis, as though he were directing a firing-squad – and then, 'the *long-range* aim,' narrowing his eyes to this more distant target, 'is to fully utilize the resources of the staff and hopefully by the end of the fiscal year to have laid stress –'

Mr Bekkus frequently misused the word 'hopefully'. He also made a point of saying 'locate' instead of 'find', 'utilize' instead of 'use', and never lost an opportunity to indicate or communicate; and would slip in a 'basically' when he felt unsure of his ground.

'– to have laid greater stress upon the capacities of certain members of the staff at present in junior positions. Since this bears heavily' – Mr Bekkus now leant forward and rested his elbows firmly on his frayed blue blotter – 'on the nature of our future work force, attention is drawn to the Director-General's directive set out in (give the document symbol here, Germaine), asking that Personnel Officers communicate the names of staff members having – what was the wording there?' He reached for a mimeographed paper in his tray.

'Imagination,' Germaine supplied.

'– imagination and abilities which could be utilized in more responsible posts.' Mr Bekkus stopped again. 'Where's Swoboda?'

'He went to deposit your pay-cheque, Mr Bekkus.'

'Well, when he comes in tell him I need the figures he's

been preparing. Better leave a space at the end, then, for numbers of vacant posts. New paragraph. Candidates should be recommended solely on the basis of outstanding personal attributes, bearing in mind the basic qualifications of an international civil servant as set forth in Part II (that's roman, Germaine) of the Staff Regulations with due regard to education, years of service, age, and administrative ability. Read that back. . . . All right. We'll set up the breakdown when Swoboda comes across with the figures. Just bang that out, then – copies all round.' Mr Bekkus was always saying 'Bang this out' or 'Dash that off' in a way that somehow minimized Germaine's role and suggested that her job was not only unexacting but even jolly.

'Yes, Mr Bekkus.' Germaine had closed her book and was searching for her extra pencil among the papers on the desk.

'You see how it is, Germaine,' said Mr Bekkus, again leaning back in the tiny office as if he owned it all. 'The Director-General is loosening things up, wants people who have ideas, individuality, not the run-of-the-mill civil servants we've been getting round here.' His gesture was apparently directed towards the outer office, which Germaine shared with Swoboda, the clerk. 'Not just people who fit in with the requirements. And he's prepared to *relax* the requirements in order to get them.'

Germaine wrinkled her forehead. 'But you did say.' She turned up her notes again.

'What did I say?' asked Mr Bekkus, turning faintly hostile.

'Here. Where it says about due regard.'

'Ah – the necessary qualifications. My dear girl, we have to talk in terms of suitable candidates. You can't take on just anybody. You wouldn't suggest that we promote people merely to be kind to them?' Since Germaine looked for a moment as if she might conceivably make such a suggestion, he added belligerently, 'Would you?'

'Oh – no.' And, having found her pencil under the Daily List of Official Documents, she added, 'Here it is.'

'Why, these are the elementary qualifications in any organization today.' Holding up one hand, he enumerated them on his outstretched fingers. 'University education' – Mr Bekkus would have been the last to minimize the importance of this in view of the years it had taken him to wrest his own degree in business administration from a reluctant provincial college. 'Administrative ability. Output. Responsibility. And leadership potential.' Having come to the end of his fingers, he appeared to dismiss the possibility of additional requirements; he had in some way contrived to make them all sound like the same thing.

'I'll leave a blank then,' said Germaine. 'At the end of the page.' She tucked her pencil in the flap of her book and left the room.

Stupid little thing, Mr Bekkus thought indulgently – even, perhaps, companionably. Germaine at any rate need not disturb herself about the new directive: she was lucky to be in the Organization at all. This was the way Mr Bekkus felt about any number of his colleagues.

'Yes, come in, Swoboda. Good. Sit down, will you, and we'll go over these. I've drafted a memo for the Section Chief to sign.'

Swoboda pulled up a chair to the corner of the desk. Swoboda was in his late thirties, slender, Slavic, with a nervous manner but quiet eyes and still hands. Having emerged from Europe after the war as a displaced person, Swoboda had no national standing and had been hired as a clerk by the Organization in its earliest days. As a local recruit he had a lower salary, fewer privileges, and a less interesting occupation than the internationally recruited members of the staff, but in 1947 he had counted himself fortunate to get a job at all. This sense of good fortune had sustained him for some time; it is possible, however, that after more than twenty years at approximately the same rank it was at last beginning to desert him.

Bekkus wanted to be fair. Swoboda made him uneasy, but Bekkus would have admitted that Swoboda could turn in good work under proper supervision. Mr Bekkus flattered himself (as he correctly expressed it) that he had supervised Swoboda pretty thoroughly during the time he had had him in his office – had organized him, in fact, for the maximum potential. Still, Swoboda made him uneasy, for there was something withdrawn about him, something that could not be brought out under proper supervision or even at the Christmas party. Bekkus would have said that Swoboda did not fully communicate.

But Bekkus wanted to be fair. Swoboda was a conscientious staff member, and the calculations he now laid on the corner of the desk represented a great deal of disagreeable work – work which Bekkus freely, though silently, admitted he would not have cared to do himself.

Bekkus lifted the first page. 'All right. And did you break down the turn-over?'

'Here, sir. The number of posts vacated each year in various grades.'

Bekkus glanced down a list headed Resignations and Retirement. 'Good God, is that all? Is this the total? How can we fit new people in if hardly anyone leaves?'

'You're looking at the sub-total. If you'll allow me.' Swoboda turned the page to another heading: Deaths and Dismissals.

'That's more like it,' said Bekkus with relief. 'This means that we can move about fifty people up each year from the Subsidiary into the Specialized grades.' (The staff was divided into these two categories, and there had been little advancement from the Subsidiary to the Specialized. Those few who had in fact managed to get promoted from the lower category were viewed by their new colleagues much as an emancipated slave must have been regarded in ancient Rome by those born free.)

'The trouble, of course,' went on Bekkus, 'is to find capable people on the existing staff. You know what the plan is, Swoboda. The D.-G. wants us to comb the Organization, to comb it thoroughly' – Bekkus made a gesture of grooming some immense shaggy animal – 'for staff members of real ability in both categories who've been passed over, keep an eye open for initiative, that kind of thing. These people – these staff members, that is – have resources which have not been fully utilized, and which *can* be utilized, Swoboda. . . .' Mr Bekkus paused, for Swoboda was looking at him with more interest and feeling than usual, then pulled himself together and added, 'within the existing framework.' The feeling and interest passed from Swoboda's expression and left no trace.

Bekkus handed back the tables. 'If you'll get Germaine to stick this in at the foot of the memo, I think we're all set. And then bring me the file on Wyatt, will you? That's A. Wyatt, in the Translation Section. I have to take it to the Board. It's a case for compulsory retirement.'

'Got one,' Algie Wyatt underlined a phrase on the page before him.

'What?' asked Lidia Korabetski, looking up from the passage she was translating.

'Contradiction in terms.' Algie was collecting contradictions in terms: to a nucleus of 'military intelligence' and 'competent authorities' he had added such discoveries as the soul of efficiency, easy virtue, enlightened self-interest, Bankers Trust, and Christian Scientist.

'What?' Lidia asked again.

'*Cultural mission*,' replied Algie, turning the page and

looking encouraged, as if he studied the document solely for such rewards as this.

Lidia and Algie were translators at the Organization. That is to say that they sat all day – with an hour off for lunch and breaks for tea – at their desks translating Organization documents out of one of the five official languages and into another. Lidia, who had been brought up in France of Russian and English parentage, translated into French from English and Russian; Algie, who was British and had lived much abroad, translated into English from French and Spanish. They made written translations only, the greater drama of the oral interpretation of debates being reserved for the Organization's simultaneous interpreters. The documents Algie and Lidia translated contained the records of meetings, the recommendations of councils, the reports of committees, the minutes of working groups, and were not all noted for economy or felicity of phrase. However, both Algie and Lidia were resourceful with words and sought to convey the purport of these documents in a faithful and unpretentious manner.

In the several years during which Lidia and Algie had shared an office at the Organization, it had often been remarked that they made an odd pair. This is frequently said of two people whose personalities are ideally complementary, as was the case in this instance. It was also commonly agreed that there was no romance between them – as is often said where there is nothing but romance, pure romance, romance only, with no distracting facts of any kind.

When Lidia first came to share his office, Algie was about fifty-five years old. He was an immense man, of great height and bulky body, whose scarlet face and slightly bloodshot blue eyes proclaimed him something of a drinker. His health having suffered in the exercise of a great capacity for life, he shifted himself about with a heaving, shambling walk and was breathless after the least exertion. When he entered the office in the morning he would stand for some seconds over his desk, apparently exhausted by the efforts, physical and mental, involved in his having arrived there. He would then let himself down, first bulging outwards like a gutted building, then folding in the middle before collapsing into his grey Organization chair. For a while he would sit there, speechless and crimson-faced and heaving like a gong-tormented sea.

Although education and upbringing had prepared him for everything except the necessity of earning his own living, this was by no means Algie's first job. During the thirties he had worked for the Foreign Office in the Balkans, but resigned in order to go to Spain as a correspondent during the Civil War. He spent most of the Second World War as an intelligence officer with the British Army in North Africa and during this time produced a creditable study on Roman remains in Libya and a highly useful Arabic phrase-book for British soldiers. After the war, his private income having dwindled to almost nothing, he entered the Organization in a dramatic escape from a possible career in the world of commerce.

It was not known how Algie came to apply to the Organization; still less how the Organization came to admit him. (It was said that his dossier had become confused with that of an eligible Malayan named Wai-lat, whose application had been unaccountably rejected.) Once in, Algie did the work required of him, overcoming a natural indolence that would have crushed other men. But he and the Organization were incompatible, and should never have been mated.

The Organization had bred, out of a staff recruited from its hundred member nations, a peculiarly anonymous variety of public official, of recognizable aspect and manner. It is a type to be seen to this very day, anxiously carrying a full briefcase or fumbling for a *laissez-passer* in airports throughout the world. In tribute to the levelling powers of Organization life, it may be said that a staff member wearing a sari or *kente* was as recognizable as one in a dark suit, and that the face below the fez was as nervously, as conscientiously Organizational as that beneath the Borsalino. The nature – what Mr Bekkus would have called the 'aim' – of the Organization was such as to attract people of character; having attracted them, it found it could not afford them, that there was no room for personalities, and that its hope for survival lay, like that of all organizations, in the subordination of individual gifts to general procedures. No new country, no new language or way of life, no marriage or involvement in war could have so effectively altered and unified the way in which these people presented themselves to the world. It was this process of subordination that was to be seen going on beneath the homburg or turban. And it was Algie's inability to submit to this process that had delivered his dossier into the hands of Mr Bekkus at the Terminations Board.

To Algie it seemed that he was constantly being asked to take leave of those senses of humour, proportion, and the ridiculous that he had carefully nurtured and refined throughout his life. He could not get used to giving, with a straight face, a continual account of himself; nor could he regard as valid a system of judging a person's usefulness by the extent of his passion for detail. He found himself in a world that required laborious explanation of matters whose very meaning, in his view, depended on their being tacitly understood. His idiosyncrasy, his unpunctuality, his persistence in crediting his superiors with precisely that intuition they lacked and envied, were almost as unwelcome at the Organization as they would have been in the commercial world. He was, in short, an exception: that very thing for which organizations make so little allowance.

Sometimes as Algie sat there in the mornings getting back

his breath, Lidia would tell him where she had been the previous evening, what she had been reading or listening to, some detail that would fill the gap since they had left the office the night before. When she did not provide these clues, it usually meant that she had been seeing a lover. She would never have mentioned such a thing to Algie, because of the romance between them.

Like many of the women who worked at the Organization, Lidia was unmarried. Unlike them, she remained so by her own choice. Years before, she had been married to an official of the Organization who had died on his way to a regional meeting of the Global Health Commission in La Paz. (His car overturned on a mountain road, and it was thought that he, like many of the delegates to the Commission, had been affected by the altitude.) Lidia had loved this husband. For some time after his death she kept to herself, and, even when this ceased to be the case, showed no inclination to remarry. She was admired by her male colleagues and much in demand as a companion, being fair-haired, slender, and not given to discussing her work out of office hours.

'Mustn't forget,' Algie now said. 'Got an appointment at two-thirty. Chap called Bekkus in Personnel.'

Lidia gave an absent-minded groan. 'Bekkus. Dreary man.'

'A bit boring.' This was the strongest criticism Algie had ever been known to make of any of his colleagues.

'Boring isn't the word,' said Lidia, although it was. She became more attentive. 'Isn't he on the Appointments and Terminations Board?'

'What's that?'

'Committee for improving our calibre.'

Algie quoted:

> 'Improvement too, the idol of the age,
> Is fed with many a victim.'

There was nothing Algie enjoyed more than the apt

quotation, whether delivered by himself or another. It gave him a momentary sensation that the world had come right; that some instant of perfect harmony had been achieved by two minds meeting, possibly across centuries. His own sources, fed by fifty years of wide and joyous reading, were in this respect inexhaustible. He had an unfashionable affection, too, for those poets whom he regarded as his contemporaries – Belloc, Chesterton, de la Mare – and would occasionally look up from his work (the reader will have gathered that looking up from his work was one of Algie's most pronounced mannerisms) to announce that 'Don John of Austria is gone by Alcalar,' or to ask 'Do you remember an Inn, Miranda?'

From all of which it will readily be seen why Algie's file was in the hands of Mr Bekkus and why Algie was not considered suitable for continued employment at the Organization. It may also be seen, however, that Algie's resources were of the kind never yet fully utilized by organization or mankind.

'Yes, here it is.' Lidia had unearthed a printed list from a yellowing stack of papers on the heating equipment beside her. 'R. Bekkus. Appointments and Terminations Board.'

'Well, I've *been* appointed,' Algie remarked, pushing his work away completely and preparing to rise to his feet, 'so perhaps it's the other thing.' He pressed his hands on the desk, heaved himself up and presently shambled off into the corridor.

Lidia went on with her work, and for fifteen minutes there was silence in the office she shared with Algie. It was a room typical of offices throughout the Organization – grey-walled, like that of Mr Bekkus, and floored with rubber tiles of a darker grey. Panels of fluorescent lighting were let into the white soundproofing that covered the ceiling. A wide low window-sill was formed by the metal covers of the radiators, and along this ledge at various intervals were stacked small sheaves of papers – the lower ones yellowing, the upper ones filmed with the grit that found its way through the aluminium window frames. (In each office the heating could be adjusted to some extent, so that in all the rooms of the Organization its international character was manifest in temperatures that ranged from nostalgic approximations of the North Sea to torrid renderings of conditions along the Zambesi.) Algie's and Lidia's desks were pushed together, facing one another, and each had a grey chair upholstered in dark blue. Blue blotters were centres on the desks and surrounded by trays of papers, black desk-sets, stapling machines, and dishes of paper clips – and, in Lidia's case, a philodendron in a cracked ceramic *cache-pot*. On each desk there was also a telephone and a small engagement pad on a metal fixture. There was a typewriter in one corner of the room, and a bookcase – into whose upper shelves dictionaries and bound documents had been crammed – stood with its back to the wall. On the lowest shelf of this bookcase were a pair of galoshes, a watering-can, an unwashed glass vase, a Wedgwood cup and saucer, three cafeteria spoons, and a single black glove.

On one wall, a calendar – the gift of a Japanese travel concern – was turned to the appropriate month (this was not always the case in Organization offices), displaying a colourful plate which bore, to Algie's delight, the legend 'Gorgeous bunch of blooming peonies'.

From the windows, which were vast and clean, one looked on to a wide river and to its industrial banks beyond. The presence of the river was refreshing, although it carried almost continuously the water traffic – coal and railway barges, tugs, tankers, and cargo vessels – of the great city in which the Organization was laid. Oceans and rivers with their simple and traditional associations of purification and continuity are excellent things to have outside office windows, and in this case helped in some measure to express that much misrepresented, highly commendable and largely unachieved thing – the aim of the Organization.

'Some bad news, I'm afraid.' Tong put his head round Lidia Korabetski's door – this was literally true, since Tong's small neat head and long neck were all of him that showed. Tong was beaming. 'Some bad news, yes.' Not naturally malicious, he had developed rapidly since entering bureaucracy.

Lidia, lifting her head, could not help asking, 'What is it?'

'Wyatt at lunch?' Tong nodded towards Algie's empty desk.

'He's been back from lunch for ages,' said Lidia defensively. Lunch at the Organization was officially one hour, and Algie was often overdue.

'They're not renewing his contract.'

'What contract?'

'His Permanent Contract, of course.' Permanence, at the Organization, was viewed in blocks of five years, and a Permanent Contract was subject to quinquennial review. 'The Terminations Board decided against renewing. They're going to let him retire early instead.'

'But he doesn't want to retire early. How unfair.'

'Another sort of place would have fired him.'

'And *another* sort of place would have promoted him.'

'Look – I like him too – everyone likes him – but there's a limit.' Limits were often proudly cited at the Organization.

Lidia took up her pencil again. 'He's a good translator.'

'Well – that's an opinion I never went along with. We worked together once, you know – on the Preliminary Survey of Intolerance. I had to correct him repeatedly.'

Lidia raised her eyebrows, but merely asked, 'Do you get full pension if you're retired before time?'

'Wouldn't be a bit surprised if he ends up better off than we do.'

'Oh come.'

'Well, at least they're not firing him. They're being decent. That's one thing you can say for the Organization. They're decent about this sort of thing. They wouldn't fire him.'

'He'd get more money if they did.' (Certain indemnities were involved in the rupture of Permanence.) Lidia put her head back down to her work. 'I've got to get on with this.'

Tong, passing Algie coming from the elevators, raised his hand in cordial greeting. 'All O.K. with you, I hope, Wyatt?' (Tong was a man who could reverse himself in this way.)

'Splendid,' grunted Algie. (Algie was a man who could grunt such a word.) He went slowly along the corridor to the office he shared with Lidia.

An odd pair, Tong thought. He still had not told the news about Algie to his friend Pike in Inland Waterways on the floor below. Rather than wait for the elevator, he opened a dangerously heavy door marked 'Sortie de Secours' and ran down the emergency stairs.

'Tong was here,' Lidia said.

'Saw him in the corridor.' Algie let himself into his chair. 'Tong,' he mused. 'The very word is like a bell.'

Lidia had no way of telling whether Algie had been informed that he was to be retired early. She would have liked to make him some show of solidarity but could only offer him a peppermint, which he refused.

'You free for lunch tomorrow?' she asked – Algie's telegraphic manner of communication having rubbed off on her to some extent.

'Tomorrow – what's tomorrow?' Algie turned several pages of his desk calendar. 'Sorry, no. Lunching with Jaspersen. Could change it, perhaps?'

'No, no,' said Lidia hastily, for Jaspersen was the one friend of Algie's who held an influential position in the Organization. 'Some other day.'

'Better make it soon,' remarked Algie – from which Lidia realized that he knew his fate.

They went on with their work in silence for some moments. Then Algie let out a snort of laughter. 'Listen to this. Chap here got it in a nutshell: "*In the year under review, assistance was rendered to sixty differing countries.*" '

Olaf Jaspersen was a year younger than Algie Wyatt and had been at Cambridge with him. People found this hard to believe, for Jaspersen was lean and fleet, his eye was clear, his features youthful. He wore dark, well-cut clothes during the week, and tweeds on Saturday mornings – which he invariably spent at the office. He had joined the Organization shortly after Algie. From the first he had been given important responsibilities, which he handled with efficiency and charm. He now held one of the most senior posts in the Organization and had established a reputation for common sense, justice, and rather more style than was usual. Things seemed to go right with Jaspersen. His career was prospering, his wife was beautiful, his children intelligent; he had even come into a small inheritance lately.

But something had happened to Olaf Jaspersen in recent years. He had fallen in love.

He had fallen in love with the Organization. Like someone who for a long time enjoys the friendship of a beautiful woman but boasts that he would not dream of having an affair with her, he had been conquered all the more completely in the end. During his early years on the staff, he had maintained his outside interests, his social pleasures – the books he read for nothing but enjoyment, the conversations he had that bore no apparent relation to his Organization duties. This state of affairs had flagged, diminished, then altogether ceased to be the case. He was still an able man, but his concept of ability had been coloured by Organization requirements; he found it harder to believe in the existence of abilities that did not directly contribute to the aim of the Organization. He was still, on occasion, gay – but his wit now sprang exclusively from Organization sources and could only be enjoyed by those in the Organizational know (of whom, fortunately for this purpose, his acquaintance had come to be principally composed). He had joined the staff because he believed sincerely, even passionately, in the importance of the Organization; that importance had latterly become indistinguishable from his own. He held, no doubt correctly, that the dissolution of the Organization would be calamitous for the human race; but one felt that the survival of the human race, should the Organization fail, would be regarded by him as a piece of downright impertinence.

Algie liked Olaf Jaspersen. He admired his many good qualities, including those gifts of energy and application which had not been bestowed upon himself. Algie's youthful memories of a lighter, livelier Jaspersen contributed to the place of the present Jaspersen in his affections. Jaspersen, in turn, had recollections of an Algie full of fun and promise, and regretted that the fun had increased in inverse ratio to the promise.

If his loyalty to Algie was in part due to Algie's never having rivalled him professionally, this was a common human weakness and need not be held against him. Jaspersen was genuinely grieved when he learned that Algie was to be retired before time, and genuinely wished to assist him. He therefore came to their lunch appointment prepared to give good advice.

The staff of the Organization took their meals in either of two places: a large and noisy cafeteria where they stood in line, or a large and noisy dining-room where they could – at additional cost – be served. The food, which was plain and good, was substantially the same in both places, although it may be said that in the dining-room the plates were slightly lighter and the forks slightly heavier. It was to the dining-room that Olaf Jaspersen took Algie for lunch this day.

Jaspersen, a man of too much taste to adopt the line of 'Well now, what's this I hear?', found it difficult to raise with Algie the delicate question of enforced resignation. In Jaspersen's view, expulsion from the Organization was a very serious matter – more serious, one might even have said, than it was to Algie himself. When Algie and he were settled with their Scotches and had ordered their respective portions of codfish cakes and chicken à la king, he bent towards Algie. 'A bad development,' he said. 'Can't tell you how sorry.'

'Ah well,' said Algie, 'not to worry.' He gave Jaspersen an appreciative nod, and went on with his drink, which he had already gone on with quite a bit.

'Rolls?' asked the waitress, wheeling up a portable oven.

'Er – one of those,' Jaspersen said.

Putting it on his plate, she identified it with the words, 'Corn muffin.'

'Mistake,' said Algie. 'Nothing but crumbs.'

'Look here, Algie, I know these fellows – on the Board, I mean. Not bad chaps – not villainous, nothing like that – but slow. Not overloaded with ideas. Only understand what's put in front of 'em. Got to be played their way or they can't grasp, you know.'

'Ah well,' said Algie again, briskly setting down his glass as if to herald a change of subject.

'Let me get you another one of those. My point is – in order to handle these chaps, you've got to get inside their minds. Talk their language.' He fished a pamphlet out of his pocket. 'I brought this for you. It's the Procedure of Appeal.' He began to hand it across the table, but at that moment the waitress came up with their lunch.

'Codfish cakes?'

'Here,' said Algie, making room. He took the pamphlet

from Jaspersen and laid it on the table beside his plate. His second drink arrived, and Jaspersen ordered half a bottle of white wine.

'The Board', Jaspersen went on, spearing a cube of chicken, 'is not the ultimate authority. That Bekkus is just a glorified clerk.'

'Point is,' Algie observed, 'he *has* been glorified.'

'I've been thinking about your case,' said Jaspersen, 'and I don't see how you could lose an appeal. I honestly don't. But get moving on it immediately – you don't have a moment to waste.'

'What year is this?' inquired Algie, turning the bottle round. 'Not at all bad.' When he had demolished the first codfish cake, he said, 'It's good of you, Olaf. But I'm not going to appeal.'

Jaspersen looked less surprised than might have been expected. 'Think it over,' was all he said.

'No,' Algie said. 'Really. Better this way.'

After a pause, Jaspersen went on kindly. 'You have, of course, exactly the sort of qualities the Organization can't cope with. With the Organization it has to be – moderation in all things. I sometimes think we should put up in the main lobby that inscription the Greeks used in their temple: "Nothing in Excess".' Jaspersen was pleased to have hit on this reconciliation of Algie's virtues with those of the Organization, for Algie was generally a pushover for the Greeks.

Algie finished another codfish cake and drank his wine, but when he replied Jaspersen was startled by the energy in his voice.

'Nothing in excess,' Algie repeated. 'But one has to understand the meaning of excess. Why should it be taken, as it seems to be these days, to refer simply to self-indulgence, or violence – or enjoyment? Wasn't it intended, don't you think, to refer to all excesses – excess of pettiness, of timorousness, of officiousness, of sententiousness, of censoriousness? Excess of stinginess or rancour? Excess of bores?' Algie went back to his vegetables for a while, and Jaspersen was again surprised when he continued. 'At the other end of that temple, there was a second inscription – "Know Thyself". Didn't mean – d'you think – that we should be mesmerized by every pettifogging detail of our composition. Meant we should understand ourselves in order to be free.' Algie laid down his knife and fork and pushed away his plate. He handed back to Jaspersen the Procedure of Appeal. 'No thanks old boy, really. Fact is, I'm not suited to it here, and from that point of view these chaps are right. You tell me to get inside their minds – but if I did that I might never find my way out again.'

'But Algie, what about your pension? Think of the risk, at your age.'

'I do get something, you know – a reduced pension, or a lump sum. And then – for someone like me, the real risk is to stay.'

After that, they talked of other things. But Jaspersen felt disturbed and sad, and his sadness was greater than he could reasonably account for.

Lidia was coming down in the elevator when Millicent Bass got in. Lidia, on her way to the cafeteria, was pressed between a saintly Indian from Political Settlements (a department high on Algie's list of contradictions in terms) and Swoboda from Personnel, who greeted her in Russian. Behind her were two young Africans, speaking French and dressed in Italian suits, a genial roly-poly Iranian, and a Paraguayan called Martinez-MacIntosh with a ginger moustache. In front of her was a young girl from the Filing Room who stood in silence with her head bowed. Her pale hair, inefficiently swept upwards, was secured by a plastic clip, so that Lidia had a close view of her slender, somewhat pathetic neck and the topmost ridges of her spinal column. The zipper of her orange wool-jersey dress had been incompletely closed, and the single hook above it was undone. Lidia was toying with the idea of drawing this to the girl's attention when the elevator doors opened at the sixteenth floor to admit Millicent Bass.

Miss Bass was a large lady with a certain presence. One felt that she was about to say 'This way please' – an impression that was fortified, when the elevator doors disclosed her, by the fact that she was standing, upright and expectant, with a document in her hand. She got in, raking the car as she did so with a hostile stare. Her mouth was firmly set, as if to keep back warmer words than those she habitually spoke, and her protuberant eyes were slightly belligerent, as if repressing tears.

Lidia knew her well, having once worked on a report for which Miss Bass was responsible. This was a Report on the Horizontal Coordination of Community Programmes, for Miss Bass was a member of the Department of Social and Anthropological Questions.

'Hello Millicent.'

'Haven't seen you for a while, Lidia.' Miss Bass squeezed in next to the girl in orange and, as far as she was able to do so, looked Lidia up and down. 'You're far too thin,' she announced. (She had the unreflective drawl of her profession, a voice loud yet exhausted.)

When the elevator disgorged them at the cafeteria, Miss Bass completed her scrutiny of Lidia. 'You spend too much money on clothes.'

Lidia was pondering the interesting fact that these two remarks, when reversed ('You are far too fat' and 'You should spend more money on clothes'), are socially impermissible, when Millicent took her off guard by suggesting they lunch together. Rather than betray herself by that fractional hesitation which bespeaks dismay, she accepted heartily. Oh God how ghastly, she said to herself, dropping a selection of forks, knives, and spoons loudly on to a tray.

As they pushed their trays along, Millicent Bass inquired, 'How much does a dress like that cost?' When Lidia was silent, she went on handsomely, 'You don't have to tell me if you don't want to.'

I know that, thought Lidia. It's being *asked* that annoys me.

'This all right for you?' Millicent asked her as they seated themselves near the windows. Lidia nodded, looking around and seeing Bekkus deep in conversation with a colleague at the adjacent table. They transferred their dishes from the tray and placed their handbags on a spare chair. Millicent also had her document, much annotated about the margins, which she pushed to the vacant side of the table. 'I was going to run through that,' she said regretfully. She unfolded a paper napkin in her lap and passed Lidia the salt. 'Those codfish cakes look good.'

Lidia began her lunch, and they exchanged casual remarks in high voices across the cafeteria din. (While talking with Miss Bass of things one did not particularly care about, one had the sensation of constantly attempting to allay her suspicions of one's true ideas and quite different interests.) Miss Bass then spoke in some detail of a new report she was working on, a survey of drainage in Polynesia. Conditions were distressing. There was much to be done. She gave examples.

'Poor things,' Lidia murmured, stoically finishing her meal.

'It's no use saying "poor things", Lidia.' Miss Bass often took it on herself to dictate the responses of others. 'Sentiment doesn't help. What's needed is know-how.'

Lidia was silent, believing that even drains cannot supplant human feeling.

'The trouble with you, Lidia, is that you respond emotionally, not pragmatically. It's a device to retain the sense of patronage. Unconscious, of course. You don't think of people like these as your *brothers.*' Miss Bass was one of those who find it easy and even gratifying to direct fraternal feelings towards large numbers of people living at great distances. Her own brother – who was shiftless and sometimes tried to borrow money from her – she had not seen for over a year. 'You don't relate to them as individuals.' In Miss Bass's mouth the very word 'individuals' denoted legions.

Lidia, casting about for a diversion, was softened to see that Mr Bekkus had brought out photographs of what appeared to be a small child and was showing them to his companion.

'Who *is* that man?' Millicent asked. 'I've seen him around for years.'

'Bekkus, from Personnel.' Lidia lowered her voice. 'He's on the Appointments and Terminations Board.'

'My baby verbalizes,' Bekkus was saying to his colleague. 'Just learning to verbalize.'

'Speaking of which,' Millicent went on, 'I hear you're losing your friend.'

Lidia hesitated, then dug her spoon into her *crème caramel.* 'You mean Algie.'

'Well, there's a limit after all,' Miss Bass said, sensing resistance.

'I'll miss him.'

Miss Bass was not to be repulsed. 'He is impossible.'

Lidia laughed. 'When people say that about Algie, it always reminds me of Bakunin.'

'One of the new translators?' asked Miss Bass, running through the names of the Russian Section in her mind.

'No, no. I mean the Russian revolutionary.'

'He's a friend of Algie's?' Millicent inquired – sharply, for politics were forbidden to the Organization staff, and a direct affiliation with them was one of the few infallible means of obtaining summary dismissal.

'He died a century ago.'

'What's he got to do with Algie?' Miss Bass was still suspicious.

'Oh – he was a big untidy man, and he once said – when someone told him he was impossible – "I shall continue to be impossible so long as those who are now possible remain possible." '

Millicent was not amused. 'The Organization cannot afford Algie Wyatt.'

'He's a luxury,' Lidia admitted.

'Pleasure-loving,' said Miss Bass, as if this were something unnatural.

'Yes,' Lidia agreed.

'And always trying to be clever.'

'That's right,' said Lidia.

'I'd prefer a more serious attitude,' said Miss Bass. And it was true; she actually would.

Lidia held her spoon poised for a moment and said seriously, 'Millicent, please don't go on about Algie. I don't like it.'

Millicent's only idea of dignity was standing on it, and she did this for some minutes. Soon, however, she forgot what had been said and inquired about the terms of Algie's retirement.

'I really don't know anything about it.' Lidia dropped her crumpled napkin on her plate.

'He has a choice, I believe – a reduced pension or a lump sum. That's the arrangement for enforced resignation.'

'I don't *know*,' said Lidia. 'Shall we go?'

When they left the cafeteria, they walked along together to the elevators.

'Now I hope you won't think me hard,' Miss Bass was beginning, when the elevator arrived – fortunately, perhaps, for her aspiration.

Algie was sitting at his desk when Lidia entered the office. They smiled at each other, and when she was seated at her desk, Lidia asked, 'Did you have a nice time with Jaspersen?'

'Splendid,' grunted Algie, going on with his work. He added, for once without looking up, 'Wanted me to appeal my case. Shan't do it, though.'

'Perhaps you ought to think about it?'

Algie shook his head, still writing. A little later he murmured aloud, 'Never more, Miranda. Never more.'

'Algie,' Lidia said, putting down her pencil. 'What do you think you'll do, then? Take a reduced pension?'

Now Algie did look up, but kept his pencil in his hand. 'No. No. Take my lump sum and look for a small house somewhere along the Mediterranean. In the south of Spain, perhaps. Málaga, or Torremolinos. Good climate, some things still fairly cheap.'

'Do you know anyone there?'

'Someone sure to turn up.' He went on with his work for a moment. 'Only thing is – it's very dangerous to die in Spain.'

'How do you mean?'

'Law insists you be buried within twenty-four hours. Doctors not allowed to open your veins. If you should happen still to be alive, you wake up and find yourself in your coffin. When my time comes, I'm going down to Gibraltar and die in safety. Very dangerous to die in Spain.'

'But what if one's really dead?'

Algie looked solemn. 'That's a risk you have to take.'

Algie died the following year at Torremolinos. He died very suddenly, of a stroke, and had no time to reach safety in Gibraltar. An obituary paragraph of some length appeared in the London *Times*, and a brief notice in the Organization's staff gazette, which misspelt his name. For so large a man, he left few material traces in the world. The slim remnants of his lump sum went to a sixteen-year-old nephew. His book on Roman remains in Libya is being re-issued by an English publisher with private means.

Just about the time of Algie's death, Lidia became engaged to a handsome Scotsman in the Political Settlements Department. Although they have since been married, Lidia has kept her job and now shares her office with a Luxembourgeois who seldom looks up from his work and confesses to having no memory for verse. No one mourned the death of Algie more than Olaf Jaspersen, who remarked that he felt as if he had lost a part of himself. Jaspersen has recently attended important conferences abroad, and has taken to coming in to the office on Sundays. Millicent Bass is being sent to Africa, and regards this as a challenge; her arrival there is being accepted in the same spirit.

Swoboda has been put forward for a promotion, but has been warned that there may be some delay. Mr Bekkus has received *his* promotion, though over some objections. He is still combing the Organization, with little success, for unutilized sources of ability and imagination. He continues to dictate letters in his characteristic style, and his baby is now verbalizing fluently along much the same lines.

Algie's last letter to Lidia was written only a few days before he died, but reached her some weeks later, as he had neglected to mark it '*Correo Aéreo*'. In this letter he reported the discovery of several new contradictions in terms and mentioned, among other things, that Piero della Francesca died on the same day that Columbus discovered America, and that there is in Mexico a rat poison called The Last Supper. Such information is hard to come by these days; now that Algie was gone, Lidia could not readily think of another source.

2. The Flowers of Sorrow

'In my country,' the great man said, looking out over hundreds of uplifted faces, 'we have a song that asks, "Will the flowers of joy ever equal the flowers of sorrow?"'

The speech, up to then, had been the customary exhortation – to uphold the Organization, to apply oneself unsparingly to one's work – and this made for an interesting change. Words like joy and, more especially, sorrow did not often find their way into that auditorium, and were particularly unlooked-for on Staff Day, when the Organization was at its most impersonal. The lifted faces – faces of a certain fatigued assiduity whose contours, dinted with the pressure of administrative detail, suggested habitual submergence beneath a flow of speeches such as this – responded with a faint, corporate quiver. Members of the staff who had been half sleeping when the words reached them were startled into little delayed actions of surprise, and blew their noses or put on their glasses - to show they had been listening. In the galleries, throats were cleared and legs recrossed. The interpreters' voices hesitated in the earphones, then accelerated to take in this departure from the Director-General's prepared text. '*Les fleurs du chagrin*', said the pretty girl in Booth No. 2; '*Las flores del dolor*', said the Spanish interpreter, with a shrug towards his assistant.

The man on the rostrum now repeated the words from the song, in his own language – and apparently for his own satisfaction, since throughout the hall only a few very blond heads nodded comprehendingly. He went on in English. 'Perhaps,' he said, 'perhaps the answer to that question is No.' Now there was a long pause. 'But we should remember that sorrow does produce flowers of its own. It is a misunderstanding always to look for joy. One's aim, rather, should be to conduct oneself so that one need never compromise one's secret integrity; so that even our sufferings may enrich us – enrich us, perhaps, most of all.' He had laid his hand across his mimeographed text, which was open at the last page, and for a moment it seemed that he meant to end the speech there. The précis-writers were still scribbling 'our sufferings may enrich us'. However, he looked down, shifted his hand, and went on. He thanked them all for continued devotion to their duties in the past year, and for the productivity illustrated by an increased flow of documentation in the five official languages. There would be no salary raise this year for the Subsidiary Category. The Pension Plan was under review by a newly appointed working group, and the proposed life-insurance scheme would be studied by an impartial committee. It was hoped to extend recreational facilities along the lines recommended by the staff representatives. . . . He greatly looked forward to another such meeting with the staff before long.

The speaker stood a few moments with his speech in his hand, inclined his head politely to applause, and withdrew. In the eyes of the world he was a personality – fearless, virtuous, remote – and the ovation continued a little longer without reference to the content of the speech, although some staff members were already filing out and others had begun their complaints while still applauding.

'Scarcely a mention of the proposed change in retirement age.' A burly Belgian youth from Forms Control gave a last angry clap as he moved into the aisle. 'And not a word about longevity increments.' This he said quite fiercely to a Canadian woman, Clelia Kingslake, who had a modest but unique reputation for submitting reports in advance of deadlines.

'That might come under the pension review,' she suggested.

'He would have said so. It's just a move to hold the whole thing over for another year.' He held the heavy glass exit door for her. The vast hallway into which they passed was brightly lit, and thickly carpeted in a golf-links green. 'And what in God's name was all that about flowers?'

They were joined by Mr Matta from Economic Cooperation. 'Yes, what was that?' Mr Matta, from the Punjab, had a high lilting voice like a Welshman's and often omitted the article. 'Has D.-G. gone off his head, I wonder?'

A group passed them heading for the elevators. Someone said violently, '. . . not even on the agenda!'

When they arrived at the escalator leading to the cafeteria, Miss Kingslake asked the two men, 'Are you coming up for tea?'

'Maybe later,' said the Belgian boy. 'Must go back to the office and see what's come in with the afternoon distribution.'

'Back to the shop, I'm afraid,' said Mr Matta from Economic Cooperation. 'Our workload has reached the point of boiling.'

Clelia Kingslake, who had greying hair and a light-grey dress, got on the moving stair alone and went up to the cafeteria.

The cafeteria was full. It usually was – and invariably after a staff meeting. Miss Kingslake joined the queue and when her turn came took a tray from the rack and a fork and spoon from the row of metal boxes. First there was a delay (someone ahead was buying containers of coffee for an entire office – a breach of good faith), and then the line moved along so quickly that she found herself at the cake before she had decided what to have. She would have preferred a single piece of bread with jam, but she had passed the butter and it would have been unthinkable to go back for it. So she took down from the glass shelf what seemed to be the largest piece of cake there. A sweet-faced Spanish woman at the tea counter fixed her up with a cup of boiling water and a tea-bag, and she paid.

She wandered out into the centre of the room looking for an empty table. There did not seem to be one, and certainly not one by the windows on the river side. She moved along beside the tables with the unfocused, purposeful step of a sleep-walker. Hot water spilled over into the saucer of her cup.

'Miss Kingslake. Miss Kingslake.'

'Oh Mr Willoughby.'

'I've got a table at the window, if someone hasn't taken it.'

'I thought you'd gone to the Field. I heard your assignment to mission went through.'

'I leave tomorrow night. But not for Santiago after all. That was changed. Let me have your tray. They're sending me to Kuala Lumpur.'

'Thanks, but I'd better not let go. I hadn't heard.'

They made their way through to the windows. She balanced her tray on a corner of his table while he cleared it of the cups, plates and tea-bags discarded by the previous occupants. When he had stacked these on the heating equipment, they sat down.

Claude Willoughby was a spare, fair-haired Anglo-Saxon who resembled nothing so much as a spar of bleached wood washed up on a beach. He was, for so industrious a man, remarkably able. He and Clelia Kingslake had been thrown together in Interim Reports, before her upgrading to Annual Reports and his lateral transfer to the World Commodity Index.

'I might –' he began.

She said at the same moment, 'I'm so glad –'

They both said, 'I'm sorry.'

'You might?' she inquired, squeezing her tea-bag and putting it in the ashtray.

'I was going to say that I might have inquired whether you really wanted to join me. You seemed to be in a trance.'

'I was afraid of seeing someone I didn't want to sit with. Instead, what a nice surprise.' She took two paper napkins from the metal dispenser on the table, and gave him one.

'You were going to say?' he asked. 'Something about being glad?'

'How glad I am, that's all, to see you before you go. I thought you must have left without saying good-bye.'

'I've been terribly busy. Forms, clearances, briefing – and of course my replacement hasn't even been appointed. They're holding the post for an African candidate – or so I'm told. And then, at home – you can imagine – all the packing and storing, added to which we've already taken the children out of school.' Mr Willoughby, having four children of school age, was a substantial beneficiary of the Staff Education Grant. 'But don't let's get into that. And of course I wouldn't have gone without saying good-bye.'

When he had said this, she stared out the window and he turned his head towards the next table, where two officials of the Department of Personnel were getting up from their coffee.

'Shouldn't have said that about the flowers,' one of them remarked – a ginger-haired Dutchman in charge of Clerical Deployment. 'Unnecessary.'

'I should think,' agreed his friend, Mr Andrada from Legal Aspects. 'If I may say so, not good for morale.'

'Particularly that part about the answer being No.'

'Isn't it curious,' Mr Willoughby said to Miss Kingslake, 'how uneasy people are made by any show of feeling in official quarters?' He placed his paper napkin under his cup to absorb spilt tea. 'I suppose they find it inconsistent. What did you think of those remarks today – I mean, about the flowers?'

Miss Kingslake was still looking out at the broad river and the wasteland of factories on its opposite bank. She held the teacup in both hands, her elbows on the table. 'I don't quite know. I think I felt heartened to hear something said merely because it was felt. Something that – wasn't even on the agenda. Still, I did find all that stuff about one's integrity a bit Nordic. After all, it would hardly be possible for most people to get through a working day without compromising their idea of themselves.'

'I think he said "*secret* integrity".' Mr Willoughby drank his tea. 'We can check it tomorrow in the Provisional Verbatim Record.'

'I suppose', she conceded, 'it would depend on how secret one was prepared to let it become.'

The noise in the cafeteria, like that of a great storm, was beyond all possibility of complaint or remedy. It was a noise in some ways restful to staff members from quiet offices, and Clelia Kingslake was one of these. Eating her cake with a fork, resting her cheek on her left hand, she looked quite at ease – more at ease, in fact, than was appropriate to her type.

'You busy at present?' Mr Willoughby asked her.

'Oh yes,' she said. (It was a question which had never in the Organization's history been known to meet with a negative reply.) 'We're finishing up the report on Methods of Enforcement.'

'How is it this year?'

'A much stronger preamble than the last issue. And some pretty tough recommendations in Appendix III.'

Someone leant over their table. 'You using this chair?'

A group of the interpreters had come in. The interpreters were always objects of interest, their work implying an immediacy denied to the rest of the staff. They stacked their manila folders on the heaters and pushed up extra chairs to the table vacated by the officers of Personnel. Two of them went to fetch tea for the entire table. The rest sat down and began to talk loudly, like children let out of the examination room.

'One could see something was coming when he looked up like that.'

'*Les fleurs du chagrin* . . . I suppose one could hardly have said *Les fleurs du mal*. . . .'

A Russian came back with a loaded tray. 'What are you laughing at?'

One of the English interpreters said, 'It would be better not to give us a prepared text at all than to make all these departures from it.'

'What did you think of the speech?' Mr Willoughby asked a white-haired Frenchman who paused to greet him.

'Most interesting.' Mr Raymond-Guiton bowed to Miss Kingslake over his tray. 'And particularly well calculated – that interpolation about the flowers.'

Miss Kingslake said, 'I rather thought that seemed extempore.'

Mr Raymond-Guiton smiled. 'Most interesting.' The repetition of the remark had the effect of diminishing its significance. He passed on with his tray and disappeared behind a screen of latticed plants.

'Now wasn't it he', Miss Kingslake asked, wrinkling up her brow, 'who refused to go to the Bastille Day party because of his aristocratic connexions?'

'You're thinking of that fat chap in the Development Section. This one's too well-bred to do a thing like that. Miss Kingslake, shall we go?'

No sooner had they risen from their chairs than two pale girls in short skirts came up with their trays of tea and cake and started to push the empty dishes aside. Miss Kingslake and Mr Willoughby lost one another briefly in the maze of tables and met again outside the glass doors, in the relative shelter of a magazine stand.

'May I see you to your elevator bank, Miss Kingslake?'

'That would be lovely,' she said.

They went down a short flight of steps and walked slowly along a grey-tiled, grey-walled corridor lined with blue doors.

'I wonder', she said, 'if we will ever meet again.'

'I have been wondering that too,' he answered without surprise. 'In a place like this there are so many partings and reunions – yet one does find one's way back to the same people again. Rather like those folk dances they organize at Christmas in the Social and Anthropological Department. I feel we shall meet.'

They reached a row of elevator doors. Mr Willoughby pushed the Up button.

She said, as if they were on a railway platform, 'Don't wait.'

'I really should get back to the office', he said, 'and see if my Travel Authorization's come in yet.'

'Of course.'

'Shall we say good-bye, then?'

'Why yes,' she said, but did not say good-bye.

A Down elevator stopped but no one got off. A messenger boy went slowly past wheeling a trolley of stiff brown envelopes.

'Miss Kingslake,' Mr Willoughby said. 'Miss Kingslake. Once, in this corridor, I wanted very much to kiss you.'

She stood with her back to the grey wall as if she took from it her protective colouring.

He smiled. 'We were on our way to the Advisory Commission on Administrative and Budgetary Questions.'

Now she smiled too, but sadly, clasping her fingers together over the handle of her bag. This prevented him from taking her hand, and he merely nodded his farewell. She had not spoken at all – he had gone quite a way down the corridor before that occurred to her. He was out of sight by the time the elevator arrived.

'Thirty-seven,' she announced, getting in.

Someone touched her shoulder. 'So good to see you, Miss Kingslake.' It was Mr Quashie from Archives.

'Oh, Mr Quashie.'

Mr Quashie, wearing a long, light-coloured robe and scrolling a document lightly between his palms, moved up to stand beside her. 'I suppose you were at the meeting?'

'I was, yes.'

'I thought the D.-G. looked tired.' Mr Quashie stepped aside to let someone get out. 'But then – I hadn't seen him since he addressed the staff last Human Dignity Day.'

'Nor had I.'

'What a job he has. One wonders how anyone stands it. No private life at all. What did you think of the speech, by the way?'

'Quite good. And you?'

'Oh – here's my floor.' Mr Quashie glanced up at the row of lighted numbers. 'I didn't hear much of it. We were busy in the office, and I stayed to answer the phones. Getting off, please. Getting off. And then I took the wrong staircase in the conference building. So I only came in at the very end. I was just in time to hear about the flowers, you know. About how we need more flowers of joy.'

3. The Meeting

Just before the meeting, which was fixed for three-thirty, Flinders took a walk in the Organization's rose garden. This garden was set in a protected angle of the buildings and looked towards the river. Seagulls – for the river was in reality part of an estuary – swooped over Flinders's head as he crunched up and down the pebbled paths between beds of wintry spikes tagged 'Queen Frederika' or 'Perfect Peace' or 'British Grenadier'. About him, plane trees scored the sky and frozen lawns rolled down to the cold river. With the exception of two uniformed guards and a statue ferociously engaged in beating swords into ploughshares, Flinders was the only human figure in sight. The grounds were closed to the public at this season, and the staff were sealed in their narrow cells, intent on the Organization's business.

Enclosed on three sides by the congested streets of a great city, the Organization was nevertheless well laid out in the ample grounds of its foundation-granted land, and stood along the banks of the river with something of the authority that characterizes Wren's buildings on the Thames at Greenwich. Here as at Greenwich the river's edge was faced with a high embankment and bordered, where the lawn ended, by a narrow walk. From this walk one looked across the river to the low-lying labyrinth of docks and factories, surmounted by an immense Frosti-Cola sign. Behind the Organization's back, the skyscrapers of the city rose as abruptly as the Alps, an ascending graph of successful commerce. The setting impressed all newcomers, and still had an effect on those members of the staff who had been with the Organization since the signing of its Founding Constitution.

Flinders, who had spent the past two years in a North African town, was all but overwhelmed by it.

A forester and agricultural conservationist, Flinders had been recruited by the Organization two years before to serve as an expert in its Project for the Reforestation of the Temperate Zone. With a single stop here at Headquarters for briefing, he had flown from his home town in Oregon to a still smaller town some hundred miles to the south of the Mediterranean. Now, on his way home with his mission at an end, he was at Headquarters once more in order to report on his work and to be – although the word was yet unknown to him – debriefed.

He had no idea of what he should say at the meeting. He had never attended meetings at all until he got involved with the Organization. His profession had kept him out of offices. His two years in North Africa could not be contained within reportable dimensions in his mind. Throughout his assignment he had, as instructed, sent in quarterly technical reports to his opposite number at Headquarters, a certain Mr Addison. These Reports on Performance in the Field (an expression which allowed Flinders to fancy himself capering in a meadow) had given a faithful account of his initial surveys, the extent and causes of erosion in the area, the sampling of soils, availability of water, and ultimately the selection and procurement of young trees and the process of their planting.

In addition, he had reported in person, as he was required to do every few weeks, to the Organization's regional office at Tangier. Apart from these trips to the coast, he had lived a solitary life. At El Attara, where the Organization had provided him with a comfortable house, he dealt with the local farmers and landowners, who were cheerful and polite, and with the local officials – who, though less cheerful, treated him well. He kept two servants and a gardener for the overgrown terraces that surrounded his little house.

In the evenings he strolled in the medina and drank mint tea in the café, or he stayed at home studying Arabic by an oil lamp. He wore the djellabah – in summer a white one, in winter one of rough brown wool. He learned to walk as the Arabs do, with a long stride designed to cover many miles, and to ride sideways on a donkey when necessary. He drove his jeep to his work in the hills, and sometimes camped at the planting sites for days at a time. At the beginning he was appallingly lonely, and for the first two months crossed off the single days on a Pan American calendar he had tacked up on his bedroom wall. But he was accustomed to an independent, outdoor existence and gradually became absorbed in his work and in the simple life of the town. The silence in the hills, the peace and variety of the countryside pleased him immensely. During his obligatory trips to Tangier, he swam in the ocean, ate French food, bought books and toothpaste, and took out an enigmatic girl named Ivy Vance who worked at the Australian Consulate. When Ivy Vance's tour of duty presently came to an end and she was posted to Manila, Flinders began to postpone even these short trips away from his work.

By the time his mission was over, he had completed not only his own assignment but also that of two other experts, once promised him as assistants, who had never materialized. No mention of this appeared in the communications he received from Mr Addison; nor did Flinders expect or wish for any. Flinders had no complaint. His salary cheques, having been afflicted by some early confusion, were arriving regularly by the second year of his stay: there was nothing to spend money on at El Attara and he saved a useful sum. Also towards the end of his mission he received full instructions for his return journey, and a large envelope containing a Briefing Kit that outlined the work for which he had been engaged and that had been omitted at the outset. Otherwise, all had gone smoothly. Mr Addison had replied to his letters with reasonable punctuality – five weeks having been the maximum delay – and had run up a creditable score of answers to questions asked. Flinders had no complaint.

Flinders had no complaint. This fact alone, had it been known, would have made him an object of curiosity in the Organization.

Two days before, on his return to Headquarters, he had met Mr Addison – a singularly small person to have been selected as opposite number to a man as tall as Flinders. Mr Addison greeted him pleasantly and introduced him to his secretary, to whom Flinders gave, for typing, a sheaf of handwritten pages containing his suggestions for conserving and extending the plantations at El Attara. The tentative inquiries he made of Mr Addison mostly seemed to fall within the competence of some other authority. Mr Addison had replied anxiously, 'Mr Rodriguez-O'Hearn will tell you about that,' or 'That belongs in the province of Mr Fong,' or 'You'd better ask Miss Singh in Official Records.' And, 'Sorry your final cheque isn't ready. Our accountant is on leave without pay.' Otherwise, all had gone smoothly.

Mr Addison explained to Flinders that he was himself under great pressure of work, at the same time producing a ticket for a guided tour of the building. The secretary to whom Flinders had handed his manuscript then showed him where to take the Down elevator and gave him a yellow slip on which was written the time and place of this afternoon's meeting.

Flinders looked at his watch, and turned back towards the main building. The gravel paths were narrow and at each of his impractical long strides his coat was clawed by Gay Flirtation or Pale Memory. His Rush Temporary Pass had not yet been issued and he was obliged to explain his business to the guard at the door, and once again at the cloakroom where he collected his brief-case and papers. It was exactly three-thirty when he took the elevator to the meeting.

Patricio Rodriguez-O'Hearn, short, bald, blue-eyed and in his fifties, came from Chile. His reserve was unusual in a man of Latin and Irish blood, but would not otherwise have been noticeable. He was calm and courteous and, since he made a policy of being accessible to his staff, often looked exhausted in the afternoons. Within DALTO – the Department of Aid to the Less Technically Oriented – he was responsible for the overseas assignments of experts. It was to Mr Rodriguez that Mr Addison and his colleagues in the Opposite Numbers Unit reported, and Mr Rodriguez reported in his turn to the Chief Coordinator of DALTO. Rodriguez had been married twice, had a number of young children, and was known to play the piano rather well. When he sat at his desk or, as at this moment, at the head of a conference table, he would occasionally follow imaginary notes with his fingers while waiting for discussion to begin.

Flinders was quite far from Rodriguez, having been placed midway down the table. A large lady sat on Flinders's right, and Addison had naturally been seated opposite. There were some fifteen other members of the meeting, and Flinders found that he was not the only expert reporting that afternoon. On his left, a shock-headed young man named Edrich, back from a three-year assignment as a Civic Coordination expert in the Eastern Mediterranean, was leafing confidently through an envelope of documents. Senior members of DALTO were taking their seats, and there were, in addition, representatives from political departments of the Organization – a thin gentleman with a tremor from the Section on Forceful Implementation of Peace Treaties, and a young woman in a sari from Peaceful Uses of Atomic Weapons. A secretary was distributing pads of white paper and stunted yellow pencils. The room was low-ceilinged, without windows, and carpeted in yellowish-green. At one end of it stood a small movie-screen and at the other a projector. At Flinders's back, a bookcase contained a 1952 *Who's Who*, and a great number of Organization documents.

Flinders, having turned to look at the bookcase, soon turned back to the table. By assuming an alert expression he tried to include himself in various conversations taking place around him, but no one paid him any attention. A young man next to Addison said, 'These problems are substantive, of course, not operational,' and Addison replied, 'Obviously.' 'Essential elements,' declared a Japanese, and 'Local infrastructure,' responded a Yugoslav. The Forceful Implementation man looked very angry, and the girl from Peaceful Uses put her hand on his arm and murmured, 'Under great pressure.' Someone else said soothingly, 'We'll put a Rush on it.'

When all the places were taken, Rodriguez-O'Hearn coughed for silence, welcomed the two experts to Headquarters, and introduced them to the meeting. The large lady leant across Flinders to ask Edrich a question, but Edrich was nodding around the table and did not see her. Edrich, Flinders noted enviously, seemed to know everybody and had greeted several people by first name. Apart from Addison, who had gone into temporary eclipse behind the leaning lady, Flinders knew no one at all.

Mr Rodriguez-O'Hearn called on Edrich to describe his work to the meeting; he then leant back in his chair and took off his glasses.

Edrich bent forward and put his glasses on. He placed on the table a list of points he had drawn up. 'I have', he said, 'recently submitted, in six copies, my final report and this will shortly be available' – he turned up another paper – 'under the document symbol E dash DALTO 604' – he glanced again at the paper in his hand – 'slash two.' He therefore proposed, he said, to give only a brief summary of his work to the present meeting, and with this in mind had prepared a list of points on which emphasis might effectively be laid. (Flinders, looking over his shoulder, saw that there were fourteen of these, on which emphasis had already been effectively laid by underlinings.) Moreover, in accordance with instructions, Edrich had brought with him a short film showing various stages of his performance in the field.

Rodriguez-O'Hearn here suggested that the film be shown first, in order to give even greater reality to Edrich's list of points. A young man was sent for who, under Edrich's supervision, set up the reel in the projector. Rodriguez shifted his chair, and Flinders, who had his elbows on the table, was asked to move back so that the lady on his right might see the screen. Edrich borrowed a ruler from the outer office, the lights were put out, and the film was set, hissing and crackling, in motion.

Flinders was immediately struck by the similarity of the opening scene to the countryside he had just left. The eroded hills, though steeper, were garlanded with terraces of vines and fruit trees and glittered white in the meridional sunshine. The village, though even smaller than El Attara, was composed of the same whitewashed houses, the same worn steps and pitted doors. At the well, the women stood talking with their jars at their feet or their children in their arms, and outside the single tavern the old men played cards. The camera wavered over flat roofs and small peeling domes and squinted at stony hills. And upon the whole, as though marking a target, Edrich's ruler now described a great circle.

'This was the deplorable condition of the area when I arrived. Low level of overall production, cottage industries static for centuries, poor communications with neighbouring towns, no telegraph or telephone system, partial electrification, dissemination of information by shepherd's rumour, little or no interest in national or international events. In short, minimal adjustment to contemporary requirements, and incomplete utilization of resources.'

Screaming with laughter, a child raced into the camera's path in pursuit of a crowd of chickens.

'As you know,' Edrich continued, 'the object of the Civic Coordination Programme is to tap the dynamics of social change in terms of local aspirations for progress. These aspirations may be difficult to establish in a society where there has been no evolution of attitudes or change in value orientation for generations and where there are no new mechanisms for action within the community structure. In order to create a dynamic growth situation resulting in effective exploitation of community potential, aspirations must be identified in relation to felt needs. The individual thus feels himself able to function as a person, at the same time participating in implementation of community goals.'

'What are the group relationships?' The lady next to Flinders sat forward tensely for the reply.

'I'm glad you ask that, Miss Bass. Owing to traditional integration of the family as a unit, the individual seems reluctant to function in a group or sub-group situation. These social patterns may take some time to break down. And this is natural.'

'Yes. This is predictable.' Miss Bass relaxed in her chair.

'Immediately after my arrival, meetings were set up with local officials to alert them to Civic Coordination projects in the vicinity and to inform them of the terms of my assignment as agreed between their own government and the Organization.' Edrich returned to the film, where a herd of shaggy goats had appeared in the main street, followed by a donkey. 'A committee was appointed to evaluate needs and resources and to establish work priorities.' The scene changed to a row of sunburnt men in dungarees and open shirts. One was leaning self-consciously on a tall staff; another was waving at the camera. 'After a certain initial language confusion – owing to a particularly corrupt dialect spoken in this region – my project was accepted enthusiastically, although a slower time-table was eventually agreed upon.'

Here the film came to a splicing, and a series of horizontal black lines twitched frantically up the screen.

'I believe the pictures will speak for themselves from here on.'

There followed, when the film resumed, a succession of scenes involving prodigious bodily labour of all kinds. One by one the men and women of the town passed across the screen – carrying great baskets of earth, digging deep and narrow ditches, or with muscles braced and heads bowed, pushing against a boulder. Once Edrich himself was glimpsed sitting on a rock and mopping his brow. And once, to the horror of Flinders, a tree was chopped down. A bridge was built, across a stream whose course was subsequently diverted. A little blockhouse of raw brick was laboriously constructed among the whitewashed domes and in no time at all bore the legend 'Administration Building' in three languages. In the final episode, every able-bodied member of the community was shown on hands and knees, breaking stones for a road that would connect the area to the nearest industrial centre.

The film came to its end in a shower of black and white flecks, and the lights were turned on. Members of the meeting got up to stretch their legs and to question Edrich about his fourteen points. A concealed fan was switched on and vibrated with a slow hum. The technician was running the film back onto its spool. Watching him, Flinders regretted that the course of events could not be similarly rewound. What of the women at the well, he wondered? What of the laughing child that somewhere on the machine spun back to his former deplorable condition – and the flock of chickens now laying their eggs in electrified coops all through the night? What improvements were being inflicted on those static industries that had for centuries repeated themselves in the graceful jars about the well?

'Coordination', the voices were insisting, and 'basic procedures'. Edrich was pulling out his chair and saying 'issue-oriented'. Flinders resisted claustrophobia: the room was like an upholstered bomb-shelter.

'You have your films with you, Mr Flinders?'

Rodriguez-O'Hearn was looking at him. Flinders brought up his brief-case from beside his chair and produced an envelope of coloured slides. 'Only a few stills, sir.'

The meeting was settling down again. He was being listened to. He knew that he cut a poor figure with his nine or ten slides, after Edrich's film. The Arabs had rather disliked being photographed, and in any case he had often forgotten to take a camera on field trips. He handed the envelope over to the technician with a sinking heart. 'They're not too clear,' he said.

Flinders had never made a speech before. He had been intimidated, too, by the eloquence of Edrich. His hands were shaking, and he placed them flat on the table before him. All the faces were turned, waiting for him to begin.

'In classical times,' he said, 'the lands bordering the Mediterranean were much more thickly vegetated. We know this, for example, from Euripides' description of the area around Thebes, or Homer's account. . . .'

Here he paused to draw breath, and the Chief of Official Records asked if he had submitted his final report.

Mr Addison confirmed that a short account of Flinders's performance in the field was at that moment with his own typist.

'But your final report, Mr Flinders,' the Records Chief persisted with thinly veiled patience. 'Your evaluation of the success of your assignment, in six copies, your recommendations for future concrete measures.'

'Given the fluidity of the situation,' Edrich put in, with a sympathetic nod to Flinders.

Flinders said slowly that the success of a mission such as his must depend on the survival of trees which had only just been planted.

The Records Chief declared that such a condition could not be regarded as an obstacle to the submission of a final report.

'One must give them a chance,' Flinders said. 'The growth of a hybrid poplar or even a eucalyptus may be very little in the first seasons.'

'A long-term project, in other words,' said Edrich.

'In other words,' Flinders agreed.

Rodriguez-O'Hearn addressed him down the table. 'Why, Mr Flinders, have we been subjected to so much erosion since classical times?'

Flinders looked at him. 'In the main, sir, it is due to over-grazing.'

Edrich said, 'Correct.'

How does *he* know it's correct? Flinders wondered irritably. He went on to speak of the movement of soil at certain elevations and in certain winds, the presence of useful or destructive insects, the receptivity of the land – all the circumstances, in fact, which had led to the selection of the trees at El Attara. 'In conditions such as these,' he said, looking along the row of fatigued faces, 'the drought-resistant species has the only hope for survival.'

'And it is this type you are concerned with?' asked Rodriguez-O'Hearn.

Flinders nodded. 'Very often these don't give dramatic results. You see – some of the most valuable types in the world are unspectacular. But they hold their own by . . . perseverance.'

The slides had been set up, and the technician asked for permission to turn out the lights. Flinders got up and stood by the screen. In the dark he could not find Edrich's ruler, and at first, being a rather awkward man, he got in the way of the picture. The slides were in colour and, although Flinders had no skill whatever as a photographer, they did derive a certain clarity from the sharp air and splendid light of the countryside.

The first slide had been taken from a hilltop; it was a panorama of the area to the south of El Attara. The contours of this country were European rather than African and Flinders had often found it possible there to imagine how France or Italy might have looked before spaciousness was diminished by overpopulation. The hills were sometimes covered by green grasses so short that after heavy rain the soil showed through in violet streaks. This picture, however, had been taken in summer, and the pebbled course of a dry stream wound through a valley of orange groves and cypress trees. The next pictures were of a depleted slope, furrowed by weather, on whose receding earth a number of sheep were pessimistically feeding.

Flinders said, 'This is the site we chose for the first plantation.'

The pictures that followed were so repetitious that he could not help wondering why he had taken them. The same hillside, and a large area nearby, were shown in various stages of preparation – but these preparations were so gradual and so little obvious to the layman that there seemed to have been no purpose in recording them.

'The work near El Attara', Flinders said, 'serves as an experiment. The country has a conservation programme now, and the local authorities have their own plans for the future.'

Someone said uneasily, 'And this is good.'

Flinders said, 'Naturally.'

Edrich called out, 'Correct.'

Rodriguez-O'Hearn's voice inquired whether Flinders spoke Arabic.

'Not very well, sir, I'm afraid.' Flinders hesitated. 'I've been studying for three years. Semitic languages are difficult for Westerners.'

'You made yourself understood, however?'

Flinders smiled. 'As to that, sir,' he said, 'how does one know?'

The last slide came on to the screen. It was a shot taken by Flinders on the morning of the first planting. Half-way up a slope, a parked truck leant inwards on a narrow, unsurfaced road. The angle of the truck was made more precarious by the ditch into which it was partly sunk and the way in which the photograph had been taken. That the truck had just stopped was evident from the cloud of white dust still rising about its wheels. Nevertheless, the gate of the truck's open back was down, and two young men in djellabahs had scrambled aboard. One was already handing down to a forest of upstretched hands the first of the small trees with which the truck was loaded. The waiting peasants – the men in brown robes, the women mostly unveiled and wrapped in the bright colours of the country folk – reached up excitedly, but the youth on the truck held the plant with extreme care. Behind him in the truck, young trees were stacked up in even rows, their roots wrapped in burlap; on the hillside above the road, dozens of small craters had already been turned in the fresh earth.

Flinders had forgotten taking the picture, although now he remembered it with a pang of nostalgic pleasure – the brilliant January morning, the shouts of delight which greeted the arrival of the loaded truck, the many serious shakings of the hand, the good omens invoked, and the long day's work that followed. He recognized all the faces in the picture – most were from the vicinity of El Attara, and a few from villages close to the planting site. Everyone in the photograph seemed to be smiling, even two children who were rolling up stones for the wheels of the truck.

A voice in the dark said, '*They* look happy, at any rate.'

The technician said, 'I guess that's all.'

The lights went on, and the slide, remaining a moment longer on the screen, grew pale. Flat and dreamlike, the hillside stood at one end of the conference room, and the reaching figures threw up their arms on an empty wall.

With a click, the picture vanished. Addison lit a cigarette. The members of the meeting were looking at their watches and speaking of appointments, perhaps thinking of their afternoon tea. A girl with flat black hair had come in and was handing a message to Rodriguez-O'Hearn. The one or two questions asked of Flinders had, he felt, little to do with what he had said, and he thought this must be his fault. Addison made an appointment to lunch with him next day, and the girl from Peaceful Uses said shyly that she looked forward to discussing with him the effects of nuclear testing in the Sahara. In the meantime, Rodriguez-O'Hearn, whom Flinders had wanted to meet, had disappeared. A secretary came in to empty the ashtrays and align the empty chairs. It occurred to Flinders that another meeting was about to take place here: the very idea was exhausting.

He left the room and walked down a grey corridor. He wished he had gone to the trouble of taking a proper film, like Edrich, or had at least prepared the right kind of final report. At El Attara he had thought these things peripheral, but here they seemed to matter most of all. He should have been able to address the meeting in its own language – that language of ends and trends, of agenda and addenda, of concrete measures in fluid situations, which he had never set himself to master. At El Attara they had needed help and he had done what he could, but he found himself unable to speak with confidence about this work. He knew the problem of erosion to be immense; and the trees, being handed down that way, had looked so few and so small.

At the elevator he met Edrich. Edrich seemed older and

shorter than he had in the conference room. Flinders would have told him what was in his heart, but he somehow felt that Edrich was not the right recipient for the information. They took the Down elevator together, and Edrich got off at the Clinic. Flinders continued to the main floor and, leaving the building by a side entrance, went out through the rose garden.

Rodriguez-O'Hearn put down the telephone. Hearing him ring off, his secretary brought him his afternoon coffee in a cardboard container.

'Thank you, Miss Shamsee.'

'Regular with sugar.' She pulled up a metal blind. In the early outside darkness, red and yellow lights were being turned on. The river icily reflected the crimson Frosti-Cola sign.

'Any other messages?'

She put a slip of paper in his calendar. 'Tomorrow afternoon, meeting at three-thirty. Two experts reporting: Suzuki in public accounting, and Raman, malaria control.'

'Better get up their files.'

'I've already sent for them.'

Rodriguez-O'Hearn drank his coffee, and made a space for the container among the papers on his blotter. He tipped back his chair. 'To think,' he said, 'Miss Shamsee, that when I was a young man I wanted to be the conductor of an orchestra.'

She took the empty container off the desk and dropped it in the waste-basket. 'That's what you are,' she said, 'in a manner of speaking.'

'No, no,' he said, but tipped his chair down again. 'Such mistakes we make,' he said.

When the girl went out he looked through his In-tray. He then wrote a note asking Addison to bring Flinders to see him the following day, signed several recommendations for new experts, and began to read a report, making notes in the margin. When his secretary next came in, however, with an armful of files, she found him looking out of the window.

'Miss Shamsee,' he said gravely, 'I'm afraid we have suffered much erosion since classical times.'

She was used to him, and merely put the files in his In-tray. She saw, as she did so, that on the edge of his blotter he had drawn a small tree.

4. Swoboda's Tragedy

It was the documents that finally got Swoboda down. His colleagues supposed that the further postponement of his promotion had been the last straw, but in fact it was the documents that did it. In the past he had been ready to carry out the often tedious duties imposed on him by the Organization – he was by nature almost too ready in this respect – but the documents finally did it. It was too much.

Like most great turning-points in life, the matter presented itself gradually. Mr Bekkus had stopped one day at Swoboda's desk and casually asked, 'Oh Swoboda, would you,' and Swoboda had said, as he had always said, 'Certainly Mr Bekkus,' and that was how it began. The arrangement was that he would send out these documents each morning, just for a few days until someone else was found to do it. The documents, which came in various related series all beginning with the symbol 'SAGG' (Services of Administration and General Guidance), then started to arrive daily, in stacks of one hundred apiece, on Swoboda's desk. He had been instructed to send them out in separate large brown envelopes to their eighty-five designated recipients throughout the Organization, in his spare time. But several factors operated against this plan. In the first place, Swoboda had no spare time. In the second place, it was impossible for him to attend to any of his normal clerical work until he had cleared the stacks of documents off his desk each morning; by then much of the day was gone and he was faced with the necessity of staying after hours. And thirdly, no attempt was ever made to find another person to cope with the documents and they were thus laid, almost literally, at Swoboda's door for ever.

Swoboda was not a brilliant man. He was a man of what used to be known as average and is now known as above-average intelligence. The years during which he might have been formally educated had been spent by him in a camp for displaced persons, but he had educated himself by observation and reflection, and had exploited to the full a natural comprehension in human affairs. He was not audacious; he lacked aptitude for self-advancement. As a member of the Social and Anthropological Department once put it, Swoboda was over-adjusted to his problem. However, if he had lost his opportunities, he had kept his self-respect. Now he felt this to be threatened. Mr Bekkus had let him down – if this expression may be used where there has been no bolstering-up. The work was not fit for Swoboda to do. It was work one might have given a deficient person in order to employ him.

At intervals in the course of his years with the Organization, commendatory remarks had been entered on Swoboda's personal file. From time to time, one of his superiors had told him that he deserved promotion – that it was a pity, even a disgrace, that nothing had been done for him by those responsible. At first, on these occasions, Swoboda had felt encouraged and had related them at home to his wife as a guarantee of advancement in the near future. Eventually, however, it became clear to him that responsibility for his promotion lay with the very officials who deplored his situation, and that they had no intention whatever of exerting themselves to the necessary extent on his behalf – having, as they imagined, dealt with the matter by proclaiming it a disgrace. Their exertions, if any, were reserved for those more insistent, less self-effacing than Swoboda. Finally grasping this situation, Swoboda declined to make life hideous for himself and those about him by constant complaint, as was the habit of so many of his colleagues. He kept his trouble to himself and sought consolation in his natural philosophy.

All the same, it hurt him. It was demoralizing. It amounted simply to this: that no one was willing to take a chance on him.

For several months Swoboda uncomplainingly sent out the SAGG documents. For several months he arrived home in the dark to find his dinner in the oven, his wife in distress, his child already in bed. If he were absent for a day, for illness or holiday, he was haunted by the certainty that a double load of documents would await him on return. During his annual vacation, an empty office on another floor had to be appropriated to house the accumulation. At last a day came when he was visited by a sensation that had been familiar to him years before, but which, even in his worst moments at the Organization, he had not re-experienced until now. And this sensation overcame his diffidence. He acted.

It was a sensation associated with his first job, in a time before he came to the Organization. Released from his DP camp, equipped with a coveted visa, sped on his way by relief committees, the young Swoboda had obtained employment in a fruit factory. Here he was to earn his first wages and his first right to call himself an independent person. This factory was to provide the slipway from which his sane new life would be launched. Here the world would make amends for his deprivation. Willing, even jubilant, Swoboda had reported for duty and punched his clock for the first time.

The section of the factory for which Swoboda had been engaged was concerned with the treatment of cherries. By the time the cherries, in vast metal trays, came to Swoboda's attention they had already been divested of stalks, stones and colour – in short, of everything that had hitherto contributed to their character as cherries. Gouged and blanched, they had then been immersed in a crimson dye so that their colour might emerge uniform. It was Swoboda's task to attach to these multitudinous, incarnadined cherries the red plastic stalks – also uniform – that would subsequently enable them to be pulled from cocktails and, as the case might be, eaten or discarded. And it was to such ends that he diligently applied himself for one long year.

The job at the fruit factory, as has been noted, was important to Swoboda. He was untrained. He had no other means of making his living in a new country – a country of whose ways he was ignorant and whose language he did not, at that time, speak with confidence. Moreover, he wished to acquit himself in the eyes of those who had assisted him. Above all, he wanted to do well in this first paid occupation.

The day he gave his notice was the happiest day of his life.

And now, amid the sheaves of documents, it all came back to him. Shaken by the same repugnance, he arrived at the same conclusion – that such work was not for the adult and civilized, not for mature and feeling persons. Swoboda did what he had never done: he took an extra half-hour at lunchtime. During this half-hour he made his way to the Bureau of Lateral Substitutions and requested transfer to another department.

Nominees for promotion at all levels were considered twice a year by a Promotions and Probations Board, and a printed list of the successful candidates was subsequently circulated throughout the Organization. Since those directly concerned were told in advance of the verdict in their case, the main interest of the list lay in keeping abreast of the fortunes of one's fellows. It is a rare heart that truly rejoices in a friend's prosperity, and it must be confessed that the offices and corridors of the Organization were swept, every six months, by gasps of indignation, of disgust and incredulity, at the revelation of the latest promotions – and by correspondingly magnified sighs of solicitude on behalf of those rejected.

Just such gusts as these were sweeping the small grey office of Mr Bekkus when Swoboda entered it on the morning of the half-yearly list. Mr Bekkus – as a member of a similar group, the Appointments and Terminations Board – was practically bound to hold his colleagues on this parallel body in low esteem. And his ill-humour was increased, that day, by the fact that he was once more faced with the task of explaining the absence of Swoboda's name from the promotion roster.

As Swoboda came into the room, Mr Bekkus was standing by the window and holding the list to the light as if to verify the evidence of his eyes.

'Claude *Willoughby*! Claude *Willoughby*!' he repeated, as if of all Claudes this was the most unsuitable. 'Cedric Sandaranayke! After this, anything's possible. Sit down, Swoboda.' Still standing in the light, Mr Bekkus turned the page and read on. 'Kenneth Eliufoo – that's geographical of course, though it won't satisfy the Africans, you can be sure of that. Paquita Vargas – well, we all know how *she* got here. . . . And I see old Marcel made it at last.' Reluctantly turning from self-punishment, he placed the list on his desk and sat down. 'Er – Swoboda,' he said, looking about his papers as if trying to recall what Swoboda was doing there.

Swoboda looked at Mr Bekkus with something more than his usual composure. It was part of Swoboda's misfortune that he pitied Mr Bekkus; that in his resistance to Mr Bekkus he was inhibited by the knowledge that Mr Bekkus was pathetic. Not that this insight was in itself supernatural – for others would have quickly arrived at the same conclusion – but what made Swoboda unusual was that he persisted in the belief even though he had spent some years in the power of Mr Bekkus and had suffered from the silliness and insensibility that constituted Mr Bekkus's pathos. By now, surely, the sense of pathos might have given way to indignation at being subordinate to such a figure. But no. Swoboda had never said to anyone, 'I'm sorry for him' (although, in the Organization, this was a recognized means of expressing contempt for an unsympathetic superior – 'I'm sorry for him, I truly am; he's pathetic' being uttered frequently and fiercely through clenched teeth). He had not even said it to himself. But in his heart he knew that Bekkus was a foolish man, a small, ignorant and pretentious man, and that he, Swoboda, was his superior in all but official rank. Swoboda was aware that Mr Bekkus had treated him ungenerously, had often been petty and unjust. He sometimes dwelt on this, almost hopefully, in his mind. But it was no use. He continued to find Mr Bekkus pathetic. And therein lay Swoboda's misfortune – one might even have said, Swoboda's tragedy.

'I suppose,' Mr Bekkus began, as if Swoboda had requested the interview, 'you will want to discuss certain factors of your situation.' Personal matters, for Bekkus, came in situations, elements and factors. When Swoboda said nothing, he went on. 'As you know, I myself have done everything possible to expedite the processing of your upgrading.' After a pause he added, 'That goes without saying.' Swoboda evidently concurred in this, for another silence fell. 'There are some very slow-thinking individuals on the Promotions Board, Swoboda. And then, when you see who *is* accepted. . . .' He lightly dashed the promotion list with the back of his hand as if Swoboda would hardly wish to make one of such a disreputable company. 'Well, we all know the delays that – ah – mitigate against rapid advancement in the junior grades. But I think I can assure you, Swoboda, that your up-grading will be followed through in the foreseeable future – that is, at the next meeting of the Board.' Mr Bekkus lowered his voice. 'This is confidential of course.'

Swoboda merely said, 'I see, sir.'

Bekkus began to be irritated with Swoboda. 'I trust, Swoboda,' he said with some severity, 'that you are not too dissatisfied?'

After a moment, Swoboda replied, 'Yes, Mr Bekkus.'

Mr Bekkus, who had been scoring his blotter with a pencil, hesitated. Before he could make up his mind whether the ambiguity of Swoboda's reply bore investigation, Swoboda himself elucidated.

'I mean, Yes, I am too dissatisfied, Mr Bekkus.'

Mr Bekkus covered his surprise with a veneer of forebearance. He even smiled – a patient smile, an administrative smile, a smile that bespoke experience and concern. 'It's natural that you should feel disappointed,' he began.

'Yes, sir.'

'But, as I've just explained to you,' continued Mr Bekkus, smiling less, 'if you take the overall view, you need *not* feel dissatisfied on a long-term basis.'

Swoboda looked steadily at Mr Bekkus. 'It is with the overall view and on the long-term basis that I feel dissatisfied,' he said.

Now it was the turn of Mr Bekkus to be silent, though he cast about with one hand in a circular gesture, as if attempting to turn the procedural wheels that had in this moment so unaccountably ground to a halt.

Swoboda went on calmly, 'And I have applied for a transfer.'

Mr Bekkus stared. Regaining the power of speech, he said, 'Words fail me.' (A poor workman will tend to blame his tools.) He emphasized the extreme gravity of the situation by putting the pencil down and folding his hands before him on the blotter. 'Swoboda,' he said very quietly, as if Swoboda were a dangerous lunatic, 'why did you do that?'

'Because', replied Swoboda, 'of the long-term basis.'

'What do you complain of? Your relationships here have been good.' Mr Bekkus took up the pencil again and began a series of ticks on his blotter. 'Your working conditions are not unpleasant.' He made a second tick. 'You got your within-grade increment.' (His tone so clearly implied 'What more do you want?' that Swoboda almost smiled.) 'Your functions have been meaningful.'

'No Mr Bekkus.'

'Do you have some specific problem?'

'The documents.'

'The documentation?' Bekkus was baffled. '*The documentation*?'

'The SAGG documents. They have become a burden. You may have noticed that.'

Bekkus shrugged. 'I have been dimly aware,' he said. It was the best description he had ever given of his general state of mind. He took up a more aggressive approach. 'This transfer, when did you request it?'

'About six weeks ago.'

'Your application – was it made verbally or just orally?' Mr Bekkus was fond of this imaginary distinction.

'I requested an interview with a Mr Yu in Lateral Substitutions.'

'But did you actually see him – visually, that is?'

Swoboda nodded. 'The matter was to be confidential until a vacancy came up. However, I prefer to tell you now.'

'I should have been consulted at the outset.' Bekkus was getting angry. 'Is this the normal procedure?'

'Yu said so.'

'What? Ah – yes. Well, I can tell you, Swoboda, that I consider this a breach of good faith on your part.' He leant forward, his eyes belligerently bright. 'Yes. After our years together – our relationship, that is – I would have liked to see some show of good faith.' He rightly implied that this spectacle would have to be provided by others: Bekkus was a victim of the ancient delusion that loyalty is to be had for nothing. 'I must tell you that I resent your behaviour in having directly approached the Bureau of Substitutions.' His voice rose. 'It was – it was –'

He's actually going to say it was an outrage, thought Swoboda, amused.

But here Swoboda misjudged Mr Bekkus, for such a simple, expressive word was not at his command. Bekkus hunted through his vocabulary – no lengthy task – for appropriate expression. At last it came. 'It was', he cried passionately, 'a – *unilateral action*.'

When Swoboda moved to the section headed by Mr Patricio Rodriguez-O'Hearn, he carried his belongings in an Out-tray. It was as radical a change as can exist within the Organization, the new section being not only in a different department but even on a different elevator bank. Mr Rodriguez-O'Hearn was Chief of Missions in DALTO, the Department of Aid to the Less Technically Oriented. The work of this department – to induce backward nations to come forward – apparently enjoyed some success, for since its inception a number of hitherto reticent countries had become very forward indeed. The department in general, and Mr Rodriguez in particular, had a relatively good reputation within the Organization, and this favourable impression had been confirmed to Swoboda in a preliminary interview.

Swoboda was scheduled to arrive C.O.D. (Commencing Official Duties) on a Monday in the middle of June, and on the morning of this day he appeared in the doorway of Mr Rodriguez's suite of offices, carrying his tray. He was received kindly by Mr Rodriguez's secretary, Miss Shamsee, who showed him into the neighbouring room he was to share with two other clerks. His possessions – a paperback Roget, a leather-framed photograph of his wife and child, an

Orlon sweater, a bottle of aspirin, and an unusually efficient stapling machine – were quickly transferred to his new desk, a blotter was found for him, and his Out-tray was re-labelled 'In'. One or two minor tasks were set him, but before he was able to begin these or take stock of the square, wide-windowed room that constituted his future premises, his new colleagues arrived.

These two men were much of Swoboda's age, and, although the yellow-haired one smiled and the dark-haired one was offhand, Swoboda formed no immediate impression of them, his mind being so full of new and nervous sensations this momentous morning. As is the way of people who are to spend many months in close company, the three of them bided their time at the outset, and the first hours passed in comparative silence. Swoboda gathered that his two new associates had already shared the office for some time, and was reassured by the fact that they were evidently on good terms.

Swoboda having been given various files to study in preparation for his new duties, it was not until the late morning of this day that he felt himself free to size up his surroundings. As he raised his head to do this, the smiling man looked up from a form on the blotter before him and, with pencil poised, inquired Swoboda's first name.

Assuming that this was required for some official purpose, Swoboda tonelessly responded, 'Stanislas.' The young man then sprang up from his chair by the window and in a moment was before Swoboda with his hand outstretched, saying 'Mordecai.' On the far side of the room the dark man also rose up from his desk, uttering the sound, 'Merv.' They all shook hands and exchanged greetings. Mordecai then took his jacket off a stand near the door and said, 'How about some lunch?'

Thus began, for Swoboda, at the age of thirty-nine, his first taste of ordinary companionship. The relations of the three men were less demanding than would have been the case with women similarly thrown together. Their work was connected only indirectly, so that most of their conversation was personal; and their personalities offered sufficient contrast to keep them interested in one another.

On Mordie's head the yellow hair stood out in a spiky halo suggesting a sun-god rather than a saint. The word 'sunny' would have come to mind in any attempt to describe Mordie, for everything about him – hair, skin, and disposition – seemed to have been touched by light and warmth. The turmoil of history and of his own circumstances had swirled about and across him – for Mordie was a grandchild of those Russian Zionists who formed the first *kibbutzim* in Palestine in the early years of this century – without taking toll of his serenity, and even seemed to have attached him the more strongly to it. Such tranquillity often includes a measure of detachment, and Mordie was somewhat like a ship that stands offshore from a beleaguered city, ready to receive survivors, to evacuate the wounded and retreating – to do, in effect, everything but participate in the conflict. This attitude of a friendly neutral did not originate in aloofness or timorousness but from Mordie's instinct for the way in which he could best be of service to his friends. Moreover, though he would not impair his usefulness by exposing it to pointless damage, it was conceivable that Mordie might yet one day suffer himself to be annihilated in some single glorious intervention.

Mervyn was in all things unlike Mordie. He was an Australian of the short and saturnine variety. His last name was Lomax and he had been born in Narrabeen, an outlying suburb of Sydney, the only son of humble but contentious parents. He had shown interest in acquiring knowledge, even while still at school, in preparation for some wider, more accomplished world which he felt sure awaited him. Since his formal instruction was limited and he had, as a youth, few like-minded companions, his self-education ranged wide, altering course almost from day to day; many subjects were touched upon, though none exhausted, and surprising gaps were left. (These arbitrary gaps subsequently contributed to an impression that Mervyn had educated himself on a desert island, by means of an *Encyclopedia Britannica* of which one volume – say, that from LORD to MUMPS – happened to be missing.)

A schoolmate, returning one day to Narrabeen from an envied trip to Europe, had informed Mervyn that the Parthenon was highly disappointing. From the vehemence with which the statement was made, Mervyn perceived that the disappointment of this youth lay with his own reaction, and that the blame had been laid upon the Parthenon as being, of the two, the more able to bear it. There followed the realization that, if beauty were not precisely in the eye of the beholder, it was at least essential for that eye to be open and favourably disposed. Mervyn's eye became in consequence so fervently well disposed that a measure of disappointment unavoidably awaited him when at last he made his appearance in the Western Hemisphere. Because of this slight disillusionment, certain of the rewards – rewards rendered for the most part in aesthetic currency – with which Mervyn's struggle for enlightenment was eventually crowned were greeted by him with defensive scepticism. He continued to court knowledge, but, like a lover once deceived, now qualified his suit with all manner of reservations and deprecation and even, from time to time, with a touch of that very hostility which had so detracted from the littoral beauties of Narrabeen.

Another anticlimax awaited him in the form of the Organization, which he joined some years later. By then, however, Mervyn was getting ready to settle, and he stayed with the Organization, though many were the misgivings he both felt and voiced. His scholastic attainments lacking academic endorsement, they had no validity whatever in the eyes of the Organization, and he was, at the time of this story, attending a third year of evening classes which were intended to culminate in a degree in Commercial Science and the right to represent himself as an educated man – a right which his time-consuming pursuit of culture had hitherto obliged him to forgo.

Swoboda, with his aptitude for such things, quickly saw that Mervyn, finding no whole and perfect world, felt himself betrayed by the ubiquitous human lapse. This was exactly the opposite of Swoboda, whose overdose of fatalism led him to value above all things the kinship of human error. The discrepancy led them into innumerable, inconclusive exchanges.

'Stan,' Mervyn would say, as they sat gingerly holding their hot containers of morning coffee, 'who are your heroes?'

'Pardon?'

'Great minds. Who?'

'Oh –' Such renderings of account were unfamiliar though not unpleasant to Swoboda. 'Kant, perhaps.'

'Kant hadn't a particle of poetry in his entire nature.'

'Newton, then?'

'Newton went wrong on Time.'

Swoboda tried another tack. 'Who are *your* great minds, Mervyn?'

'Ah,' Mervyn began to rub his left hand absent-mindedly up and down his lapel, caressing his heart like an old wound. 'There are no great minds, Stan,' he said sadly. To be great, in Mervyn's opinion, was to be infallible.

Both Mordie and Mervyn were somewhat senior in grade to Swoboda, and both had encountered Mr Bekkus during their careers at the Organization.

'I bet Bekkus blighted your life,' Mervyn remarked one day.

Swoboda's reserve would have produced some non-committal reply, had Mordie not seconded this view. 'Ah – Bekkus. I too recall him as a Life-blighter. How long were you in his office?'

'Nearly four years. Ever since Specific Cases Unit was merged with Overall Policy.'

'Christ, Stan, why did you stick it?'

There was no answer to this – unless Swoboda were to allude to the nature of his tragedy. Slowly, however, his life with Mr Bekkus was unfolded to his new friends. Mordie and Mervyn were able to size up the situation in their respective ways and to savour the triumph of Swoboda's final interview with Mr Bekkus.

'Stanislas, you did right.'

'Good on you, Stan.'

'Not', went on Swoboda, 'that we parted on bad terms. That, indeed, would have introduced a new sincerity into our relations. Far from it. Not knowing my new telephone extension, Mr Bekkus pointed out that I should have to call him in order for us to, as he put it, get together.'

'And will you?'

Swoboda paused. 'On my last day, Mr Bekkus walked with me to the elevator. He put his hand on my back and said "Remember, Swoboda, it will be your fault if we don't get together soon."'

'What did you say?'

Swoboda smiled modestly. 'I said – "That's right."'

Mordie's smile shot up to his ears.

Mervyn slapped his hand on the desk. 'Stan the Man! The *Original* Man!'

Mordie said, 'Stanislas, I confess to a pleasant surprise.'

'You would have expected me to weaken?'

'Not exactly. But I thought perhaps you are one of those who gives in for the good old times' sake.'

'That expression, Mordie,' said Mervyn, 'is "*for old times' sake*". Nobody ever said it was *good* old times' sake.'

Swoboda was also kindly treated by Miss Shamsee and, though he saw less of her than of Mordie and Merv, not a day passed without his exchanging some friendly words with her or consulting her about his work.

Miss Shamsee had been ten years with the Organization and was now a little over thirty. Her face had the gloss of a ripe olive. Her black hair was flat, parted in the middle and drawn back in an immaculate knot. She invariably wore a sari – sometimes a beautifully bright one, sometimes a drab and flimsy one – and this graceful garment contributed a stateliness, though she was not tall. She had a remarkable walk – it was the curving, sinuous walk of Hazlitt's Sally Walker – which, combined with the semicircular folds of her dress, gave her an effect of coiling and uncoiling as she passed through offices and down corridors, as she glided between filing cabinets or along cafeteria queues.

In addition to these physical advantages, Miss Shamsee possessed a good mind and pleasant manner. She should, by any fair standard, have been an attractive woman; yet it cannot be said that she was. All the elements were there, but Miss Shamsee was like a resort town in bad weather: some spark, some animation, some synthesizing glow was missing. She had been too long with the Organization.

Girls like Miss Shamsee pursued, year in, year out, their stenographic or clerical duties at the Organization, and were to be seen each day lunching in the cafeteria with two or three of their kind. Their salaries were low, but every year they earned a little more money, and every ten years or so they went up a notch in the clerical scale. No professional advancement was offered them, except over such a length of time as to invalidate it. Marriages were rare, resignations even rarer (for, somewhere about the age of twenty-seven, they started to be concerned over the drawing of their eventual pension). If fortunate, they might be assigned to one or two Organizational meetings abroad; if desperate, they mighty apply for long-term service in the less technically oriented lands.

The previous year, Miss Shamsee had been sent to the Organization's branch office in Geneva to assist at a summit conference of the less technically oriented. There she had met and fallen in love with an official of the World Geophysical Union, an international agency affiliated with the Organization. The man was married, and Miss Shamsee's assignment was for six weeks only, but the affair was poignant and sincere. Towards the end of the conference they arranged, by intricate deceptions, to go away together for a brief time. (In this they were aided by the Organization holiday of Self-Determination Day, which, falling on a Monday, provided a long week-end.) Other cities in Switzerland being rendered perilous to them by the various headquarters of agencies of the Organization (the Global Health Commission at Lausanne, the Bureau of Legal Standards at Berne, and so on), and the Riviera being out of the question owing to a large Organization-sponsored Poverty Congress then in progress at Cannes, they decided on Milan as the neighbouring city least fraught with international aspirations. There they duly arrived by train and stayed at a large old-fashioned hotel near the station.

These days were to be the most inspiring of Miss Shamsee's life. She and the geophysicist walked about the city in a kind of trance, with arms linked. Although it was May, the weather was cold and Miss Shamsee wore a cardigan over her sari, and a grey woollen coat she had bought on sale in the *Grand Passage* in Geneva; ankle socks kept her feet warm in her sandals. Even thus modified, her rippling walk attracted much favourable attention. The air was filled by the spring seeding of the great poplar forests of the Lombardy Plain, with the result that tufts of soft white down fell throughout the city like a gentle, continuous snow. This, and the unexpectedness of sudden love, made the situation seem fantastic and spiritual.

Their respective shares of the hotel bill having been carefully calculated by the geophysicist, they returned to Geneva by separate trains, and met only once more, for the following day was Miss Shamsee's last on full *per diem*; she was due to fly back to Organization Headquarters that evening. They said good-bye in the Contemplation Room, where they could be sure of not meeting anyone they knew. The geophysicist asked her not to write to him. In her heart she knew this to be abject, but she gave him a look of understanding so as not to spoil things. They parted without touching. Thus ended Miss Shamsee's meeting at the summit.

Back at Headquarters, she did not repine. She was deeply moved, but triumphant. This at least had happened to her. Though she said nothing, it gradually became known that something of the kind had occurred, and it gave her prestige among her sad companions. Once in a while, when Mr Rodriguez-O'Hearn dictated a letter to the World Geophysical Union, she could allow herself to think that her lowercase initials in the corner of the page might act as a message to her lover – that somehow, eventually, they might come to his attention as he thumbed through the relevant file. And one day at the beginning of winter, when for the first time she hung up her grey coat in the office, she found a scrap of white poplar-down in the sleeve. She pressed it that day in the Organization Yearbook.

Swoboda discovered, through his companions, the varying degrees of esteem in which the rest of the DALTO staff were held – who was to be relied upon, who to be supported, who avoided. He also learnt of the existence of one or two natural enemies.

'Take a dekko at this,' Mervyn would say, holding up a sheaf of memoranda, each marked with a red HASTE sticker. 'Bloody Battle of Hastings.'

'Sadie Graine, I suppose?' inquired Mordie. Miss Sadie Graine was the secretary of DALTO's Chief Coordinator, Mr Achilles Pylos.

Swoboda, who as yet knew the lady only by sight, dwelt on her name. 'Sadie. I didn't think women were called Sadie any more.'

'Short for "Sadist",' Mervyn explained, sorting out the papers. 'Affectionate diminutive.'

(This is not the moment to relate in full the story of Miss Sadie Graine. In the history of the Organization, as in the annals of all organizations, that narrative has a place – for Miss Graine's is a figure known in all large institutions, and even in some smaller ones. Her presence in any substantial office is as inevitable as that of filing cabinets and paper-clips; no departmental scene is complete without her. Her own position is subordinate, yet she commands, fearfully, inexplicably, the ear of authority. She accepts no criticism, she possesses no humour; her tyranny is self-righteous, her vengeance inexorable. The sole – and unwitting – contribution made by her presence is to join together those who would otherwise find no common ground. For concerning Miss Graine there can be no divergence of opinion. Before her, all stand united in adversity.

The story of Miss Sadie Graine may yet be told.)

In the new comradeship enjoyed by Swoboda, there was one element more remarkable, more sympathetic than all the others. And that was the bond that developed between Swoboda and Mr Rodriguez-O'Hearn.

Mr Rodriguez-O'Hearn was, at the age of fifty-three, one of the most senior officials in DALTO. He was not the

Chief Coordinator of the department – that office being filled by Mr Pylos – and his secondary position was shared with two or three others. Still, he was a person of authority by Organization standards – and more ample standards might only have augmented his prestige.

The accidents of politics and geography which sometimes united to provide the Organization with its higher officials had seldom combined so happily as in the case of Mr Rodriguez-O'Hearn. His was a mind of uncommon scope and flexibility. He was humorous, compassionate, and incorruptible – these invaluable qualities being here listed by order of importance. His sensibilities revealed themselves, as sensibilities will, continually; and not least in his mannerism of fingering a piece of music from time to time on an imaginary piano. And he was, to a degree unusual in the Organization, a cultivated man. There was, one felt, almost nothing he might not have done.

Yet Mr Rodriguez-O'Hearn had colleagues of less ability who had gone further; of less energy who had done more.

In all Swoboda's years with the Organization he had not encountered any official of this calibre. His natural kinship with Rodriguez-O'Hearn went beyond that which he enjoyed with Mervyn, Mordie and Miss Shamsee. Admiring as Swoboda was of Rodriguez's gifts, he was also drawn to him by the inconsistencies he began to detect under Rodriguez's thoughtful exterior.

Confronted, for example, with some Daltonian dilemma, Rodriguez could instantly see what should be done. He would perhaps ask Swoboda to prepare such-and-such a draft memorandum to that effect. Swoboda would do so but, by the time the draft had reached the In-tray, a dozen fanciful doubts had been raised in Rodriguez's mind and a dozen spectres of possible misfire sat about Rodriguez at his desk. The strength of the doubts appeared to be in direct ratio to the significance of the issue and the clarity of the proposed solution. 'Thinking it over, Swoboda,' Rodriguez would say, 'I feel we should add . . .' Swoboda began to dread these final paragraphs, these postscripts or parenthetical observations that so often merely served to draw attention to potential errors that would never otherwise have been committed. 'Perhaps it should be pointed out' or 'I need hardly warn the members of the committee' or, worst of all, 'In order to avoid confusion' frequently preceded a knockout blow to the argument so lucidly adduced in the body of the letter.

Caution, concluded Swoboda, is a very dangerous thing.

There were, in addition, issues that Rodriguez would perpetually and ignominiously evade rather than oppose – a multiplicity of useless regulations, an inundation of documents whose pages were more commonly committed to the wastepaper basket than to memory, the infringements of troublesome subordinates, the harassments of Miss Sadie Graine. (It would not have been accurate to say that Mr Rodriguez-O'Hearn was afraid of Miss Sadie Graine, but it would have been so nearly accurate that it did not quite bear thinking about.)

Rodriguez had a peculiarity, too, of gratifying – almost of acting out – another's misunderstanding of him. With those who thought him unyielding, he would be at his most taciturn; with those who thought him irresolute, at his most discursive. Swoboda saw these things and, feeling he understood the matter, regretted them. Yet it cannot be said that they lowered Rodriguez-O'Hearn in Swoboda's regard. They were authentic human aberrations, and Swoboda's tolerance of them only increased the friendship which, for all its restraint, gradually grew up between him and his new chief.

Swoboda had come to Rodriguez-O'Hearn as a virtually unknown quantity. It is true that his personal file had been sent to Rodriguez in advance, and that these dossiers were compiled in conformity with the latest administrative techniques. A form in the file had accordingly notified Mr Rodriguez that Swoboda was punctual and in good health, that he upheld the aims of the Organization, and that his output was high. The form was composed as a questionnaire, and against each question a series of boxes invited the appropriate tick – such methods as these having been painstakingly devised in order to avoid anything resembling a personal opinion. Since, in this modern world of incomparables, a tick in anything less than the topmost box for each item would have been highly damaging to a staff member, Rodriguez-O'Hearn also learnt – and expected to learn – from the file that Swoboda was of ineffable good humour, that his initiative was unremitting, his imagination inexhaustible, and his judgement invariably sound. Had the file contained a more reasonable estimate of Swoboda's capabilities or suggested the slightest singularity, the implication would have been such that neither Rodriguez-O'Hearn nor any other Organization official would have felt justified in accepting him.

It was therefore without prompting of any kind that Rodriguez discovered Swoboda's true nature. Rodriguez was a man of insight, and the significant outlines of Swoboda's past gradually became as apparent to him as if he had been informed of them in detail. He valued Swoboda's industry; he respected Swoboda's discretion; he even came, little by little, to apprehend Swoboda's tragedy.

And so it came about that Swoboda thrived. With all his new colleagues he worked in the utmost goodwill. There was much to do, but no injustice corresponding to the SAGG documents darkened Swoboda's days or lengthened his nights. His tendencies, though orderly, were ingenious, and he developed an uncomplicated system of shading in the progress of DALTO operations on the graphs entrusted to his care (so many experts sent to instruct needy nations, so many grants awarded to the less technical for orientation abroad – their shadow, on Swoboda's charts, never grew less). Together with Mervyn and Mordie he drafted letters, added up columns, and filed cards. There was nothing novel or intriguing in this, other than the sense of being appreciated. All the same, Swoboda felt his life was moving forward again and, in his modest way, he was hopeful about the future.

Towards the end of the year, when Swoboda had been some months with DALTO, the question of his promotion was once more raised in his mind. The Board was soon due to hand down its six-monthly decisions. He mentioned this to Merv and Mordie.

'You'll be all right,' Mervyn assured him. 'He likes you.'

'Who?'

'Old Rodrigo. Can't think why, but he does.'

'What has he to do with it?'

'He'll have to endorse you. That's what happens when you move to another department. You have to get put up again for promotion by your new chief.'

'It's a formality,' Mordie said. 'They'll bring it to his attention. Don't worry.'

A week or two later, Miss Shamsee whispered to Swoboda that Rodriguez had dictated to her the recommendation for promotion. Smiling, she showed Swoboda a page of cryptograms. 'One of the best recommendations he's ever given,' she said. 'It's marvellous.'

Swoboda thanked her, warmly but calmly, and walked away. In that moment, however, he was as close as he had ever been to exultation. He went down to the cafeteria and had a cup of coffee. There, leaning on the Formica table-top, absently stirring the sugar round in his thick cup and crumbling his Danish, Swoboda reflected on the goodness and ultimate meaning of things. How right he had been to stand up to Mr Bekkus. There was much in life that one must let pass, much that did not merit the taking of positions or the agitating of one's breast; much, in fact, that it would be demeaning to take issue with. On the other hand, certain matters were not to be ignored unless one were to cast oneself away entirely, and here Swoboda had vindicated himself. He had repudiated Mr Bekkus's treatment of him; he had demanded a more suitable standing in the world, and he had got it. He had, through his own fortitude, come forth into a new life of comradeship and esteem. He would receive a little more money, he would stand a little higher in the lowly lists of the Subsidiary Category. Swoboda was content. (It may be felt that he was easily content, but he is not the less to be envied for that reason.)

In a sense, too – or so it seemed to him – the Organization itself stood to profit from this development. Having dedicated itself to the rights of man, the Organization was, in some subtly heartening manner, only as good as the way it treated Swoboda. One could not completely believe in any enterprise that required one's own diminution.

Thus Swoboda, as he lingered over his coffee in the cafeteria. Not since the departure from the cherry factory had his heart been so light.

The days passed quickly at the end of the year. There was great activity in DALTO at that time. The deadline for submission of the DALTO annual report was drawing near, and Swoboda with his charts was deeply involved. As this vast report required some months in the preparation, it was always begun in the middle of the year it purported to cover. Necessarily incorporating an element of conjecture, it was an earnest effort for all that. It was Swoboda's first experience of the reporting strategy and he was quick to grasp its tactics of defence: a programme, for example, was 'particularly' efficient; a situation had been 'carefully' examined; a success was 'outstandingly' successful – these adverbial badges of insecurity being designed to take the opponent by surprise.

Swoboda's normal work was disrupted by the report, but he was assured that this was a temporary inconvenience and he did not mind. Cheerfully he pieced together the scissored paragraphs ('Two experts in metallurgy served in Tanzania during the year under review . . .' 'Four awards were made for the study of sanitary engineering abroad . . .' 'A fruit factory was erected in Kashmir . . .'). Swoboda was surprised to see how the very items that had been the subject of so much anxiety and dispute throughout the year appeared, when reported, to be part of some grand and faultless design to which no disharmony could ever conceivably have attached. He tried to reflect that this was perhaps, in some final and overwhelming sense, no more than the truth.

In the days before Christmas, the long corridors of the Organization were gay with plastic wreaths, and in the main lobby the Organization Singers chanted carols interspersed with the Founding Constitution set to music. It was on the afternoon of the DALTO Christmas party that Mr Rodriguez-O'Hearn asked Swoboda to come into his office. Swoboda was, of course, in and out of Rodriguez's office all through the working day; but there is an atmosphere, a closing of doors, a lowering of voices, a pushing away of papers, that unmistakably announces an interview of more personal character. (I am sorry to say that, although such interviews do occasionally bring good tidings, their general climate is one of foreboding.) Swoboda assumed of course, and rightly, that the discussion would have to do with the matter of his promotion, which he had been expecting Rodriguez to mention. It was known that the Board would soon meet – perhaps it had even met already, and Rodriguez was now authorized to give Swoboda the good news.

'Swoboda, sit down,' said Mr Rodriguez-O'Hearn. He

performed a scale or two with the fingers of his right hand and said nothing more for some moments. Swoboda was oddly reminded of Mr Bekkus. But he put this out of his mind with a dismissing mental smile.

'Swoboda,' Mr Rodriguez said again, 'I'm sure you know that I have the highest opinion of your work.' He was looking not at Swoboda but at his own right hand, which was now executing more complicated fingering. 'And, I may say, of your character.' He then interpolated, 'The two cannot, in any case, be separated.'

Swoboda did not speak. He observed Rodriguez carefully. He was interested in human nature and his intuition told him that he was getting an important demonstration of it.

'You must be aware,' Rodriguez went on, now looking briefly at Swoboda out of his fine blue eyes, 'that the question of your promotion was due to come before the present meeting of the Promotions and Probations Board. And that my endorsement was required.'

'Yes, sir.'

'Quite so. Well, Swoboda,' here Rodriguez stopped. Swoboda, watching him, wondered what word should be used to describe his expression. He decided that the most fitting word was 'desperate'. Rodriguez then continued. 'I did in fact write the recommendation on your case. And I may say that it was unequivocal. It was, indeed, wholehearted. However –'

'However?' Swoboda inquired gently, since silence seemed likely to descend.

'However – some questions were subsequently raised. I mean, after I had drafted the report on you. It was felt that, since you had joined this department so recently, others here might feel – ah – supplanted in the matter of your promotion. I do not say that I agree with this view, but it was presented to me as a possible source of grievance. . . . Miss – er – Graine did in fact raise the matter with Mr Pylos, or so I understand, and he felt. . . . Then, too, an official of Personnel – Mr Bekkus, in whose office you formerly worked – seems to have said . . .' Rodriguez-O'Hearn's voice trailed away. He summoned it back and added more firmly, even defiantly, 'And so, taking all these things into account, I did not send my recommendation.'

'I see, sir.'

'Swoboda,' said Mr Rodriguez-O'Hearn – and Swoboda now concluded that the word for his expression was 'hopeless' – 'this doesn't mean anything more than postponement. You realize that, of course.'

'I see, sir,' Swoboda repeated. He was still looking at Rodriguez-O'Hearn – at his expression, his rapidly heaving chest, his intricately moving fingers. A sensation was welling up within Swoboda as he looked, and this sensation, though he struggled against it, held him fast and threatened to overcome him.

'In fact I think I can safely say that at the next meeting of the Board – that is, the one after the present one – the one that meets in June – this is confidential, of course. . . .'

Mr Rodriguez's voice halted, wandered on. Swoboda sat still. Soon he would rise and go. Was there not the Christmas party to attend, and had he not promised Abdul Karim of Fellowships to help him serve the drinks? There was nothing to stay for here, nothing more to be said, even though Mr Rodriguez was still talking, for Swoboda had now surrendered to the familiar feelings that had assailed him in the past few moments. He had fought against them, but to no avail. Try as he would, Swoboda could not change; he could not help himself. There was nothing to be done about it. The fact was that he pitied Mr Patricio Rodriguez-O'Hearn. He pitied him with all his heart.

It was nothing short of tragic.

5. The Story of Miss Sadie Graine

The moment his new secretary was introduced to him, Pylos knew it would not do. He looked at Miss Sadie Graine and, even as he smiled and shook her hand, he knew that it would not do. It was his first day at the Organization and, although his appointment was a lofty one, he did not wish to begin with a complaint. But the next day, or the following one at latest, he would ask for a different secretary.

Miss Sadie Graine was a tiny woman. She was barely five feet tall. Her features and bones were bird-like, her head tightly feathered in grey. She was an angular little creature, sharp of nose, eye and tongue; but her lips were her most singular characteristic, being in repose (though that is not the word) no more than a small straight line. People meeting Miss Graine for the first time were apt to exclaim afterwards, 'But the mouth. My God, the *mouth*.'

It had not always been so. There existed, in fact, a childhood photograph from which a tiny Sadie gazed forth with eyes large and luminous. These eyes – from taking in less and less, from peering ever harder into ever narrowing interstices – had contracted to their present dimensions. It is not the purpose here to study the causes for shrinkage. (Causes there were, for Sadie Graine's story was, like everybody's, a tale of truth and consequences.) Miss Graine's tale will rather be told in the form – the outmoded and discredited form – of her effect on others.

Achilles Pylos was a Greek, and it gave him a pang to see what had become of this woman of the Western world. Had the faces of certain male colleagues been pointed out to him as correspondingly ravaged, he would have replied that, in the case of a woman, a more aesthetically pleasing article had been despoiled. For Mr Pylos was well-disposed towards women. His own wife was beautiful. He was prepared to discover beauty in almost any woman, and it depressed him when, as in the case of Sadie Graine, he was utterly thwarted. It must not be thought, however, that Pylos recoiled from Miss Graine merely for her lack of looks: he was not a profound man but he was not entirely superficial and his glance penetrated at least as far as the upper substrata of Miss Graine's configuration. His own nature, beneath its meridional pretentions, was an easy-going one, and he knew that he could not keep Miss Sadie Graine.

Miss Graine returned his smile with one of her own so pointedly summoned just for him that it seemed to seal her off from the others in the room – his new administrative chief, a flannel-suited man called Choudhury, and his fiscal officer, a Mr Chai. Miss Graine was wearing a coat and skirt, and a blouse so unfrivolous that it at once suggested the absence of a tie. Mr Pylos fleetingly took in these details as he walked across his new office to the windows (of which, since the room was a rather grand one by Organization standards, there were three). His token gesture towards pulling up the venetian blinds brought the others quickly to his side, and in a moment he was looking down some thirty storeys to the Organization gardens below. He was unused to great heights, and steeled himself to a vertiginous future.

'This will be the West, I suppose?'

'The East,' corrected Chai. 'Or so I believe.'

'Ah – the East. Of course.' Pylos bravely kept his eyes on the scene below. 'And these are the gardens,' he went on, not risking further conjecture.

'The gardens,' Choudhury agreed. 'Yes.'

'Is that something being built down there? Or demolished, perhaps?'

'Where, sir?' They all leant forward to see.

'There. Near that clump of trees.'

'I don't quite – Ah yes. Yes, of course. No, that's a sculpture, sir. The gift of Denmark, I think. Or is it the Netherlands? I can easily find out if –'

'No, no, just curiosity. Yes, I see now. Very modern, of course. Very – er – er.' Pylos waved a well-kept hand.

'Very *free*,' Choudhury supplied.

'Free, yes,' Pylos echoed, taking the opportunity to liberate himself from the window. 'Now where does this lead?' He strode across the bright blue carpet and got a shock when he laid his hand on the metal knob of a door.

'The carpet, you see, sir. That's what does it,' Miss Graine pointed out. 'It's the electricity in the carpet.'

Chai hurriedly explained about the door. 'That's your conference-room, sir. There are three doors, as you see – the one to your outer office, this to the conference-room, and the other leads to – er – Miss Graine.'

But not for long, Pylos added reassuringly to himself. 'Well, gentlemen,' he said, going behind his desk and standing there with his fingertips resting on the blotter, 'this all seems very satisfactory. It will take me a while, naturally, to. . . .'

'Naturally' and 'Of course' came readily from the lips of his two subordinates. 'If in any way,' they said, and 'Any thing at all.' Miss Graine all the while stood by, and Pylos had the impression that she was waiting for the others to leave. He therefore said, 'And now, since I understand I have a busy afternoon of meetings, I'd like to get on with these' – he laid his hand on a pile of documents with which he had been provided (the Founding Constitution of the Organization, the Basic Legislation Governing Extension of Aid, the Standard Conditions of Application) – 'interesting papers.' He smiled as if his thoughts were already elsewhere, and kept smiling like that until he had the room to himself.

Pylos sat down at his desk and really looked at everything

for the first time. There were more gadgets than in his previous office, in a ministry in Athens – two telephones, each with a battery of numbered buttons, a small transmitter for the relaying of debates from Organization auditoriums (an arrow on the dial of this device could be turned to any of the several languages into which discussions were interpreted), and an intercom freshly marked 'Miss Graine'. Otherwise, the room did bear a certain bureaucratic resemblance to his former premises, and he really had to remind himself that beyond these walls lay no prospect of the Acropolis or Mount Lycabettus but a dizzy panorama of the peaks and ledges of immense office buildings.

As he sat with his hands folded on the immaculate blue blotter, he could not help wondering again how he came to be there. The new department that Pylos had been asked to head – a body to aid impoverished areas of the world – had been formed as a result of recent Organizational deliberations. Barely two months had passed since Pylos had received in Athens the cable offering him the post of Chief Coordinator in this new department. The conditions seemed not unfavourable, the salary – when translated into drachmae and calculated together with allowances – not ungenerous. His Athenian post in foreign affairs was soon relinquished (with satisfactory arrangements made to perpetuate his pension rights); his furniture was soon crated, his bags soon packed, his colleagues envious, his wife overjoyed. On the ship he carefully studied the Organization papers that had been sent to him, and he and his wife read aloud to one another from the *Reader's Digest* in order to improve their English. To no one, however, did Pylos express the surprise he felt: he was too much a Greek for that. He assumed it would eventually become clear to him how he, Achilles Pylos, a civil servant with no Organizational connexions, with the merest smattering of knowledge in economics, should have been chosen for this post. He did not worry unduly about his suitability: he had been a bureaucrat too long for that. But he determined to go quietly until he got the lay of the Organizational terrain.

The matter was in fact a simple one. When the Organization's Governing Body created a department to aid retarded nations, the question of a chief for that department instantly arose. He must be a national of a certain kind of country – a country not too contrastingly prosperous, yet not conspicuously delinquent; a country with an acceptable past, a decently uncomfortable present, and a reasonably predictable future. The man, likewise, must walk the middle path – a man of middle years and middle brow was wanted, a man not burdened with significant characteristics. Certain governments were asked to suggest candidates. Some sent the names of those they wished to be rid of, some proposed the ancient or the controversial. There were candidates who spoke no English, candidates who were chronically ill. One or two were over-qualified and would have made trouble by taking up positions. A committee deliberated. The field was narrowed. At last the word went round. 'They're trying to dig up a Greek.'

Some weeks of archaeological jokes and official indecision were followed by the announcement of Pylos's appointment. The staff of the new department – who had all been drawn from other areas of the Organization – at first rejoiced, without knowing why. In Organization circles, the devil you don't know is always preferable, and it was readily believed that Pylos was a man of outstanding talents. Rumours circulated that he had been a hero of the Greek Resistance, that he possessed a famous collection of antiquities, that his wife owned a shipping line, that he had come to prominence from poverty-stricken origins, that his family was a princely and immensely rich one. At last, as his arrival drew near, the staff reconciled themselves to reality. Their reception of the real Pylos had nothing to do with the legends that preceded him, for in their hearts they had known all along how closely he would resemble his peers. So close, indeed, was this resemblance that the official sent by the Organization to meet Pylos at the dock picked him out at once from a throng of fellow-passengers.

And now, alone in his new room, still wondering what particular quality of his had struck the Organizational hierarchy, Pylos could not know that it was precisely his lack of striking qualities that had brought him there.

He got up and went over a second time to the closed door that led to his conference-room. Taking out his handkerchief, he turned the metal handle cautiously. At this moment a single knock was instantly followed by the opening of another door, and Miss Sadie Graine came into the room.

Pylos smiled again at Sadie Graine. The sooner she goes the better, he thought, putting away his handkerchief. But he came – as it were, obediently – back to his desk where she stood, and sat down.

'I've prepared a list of your meetings this afternoon,' said Miss Graine, placing this on the corner of the desk.

Pylos drew the paper towards him and saw that it was, in fact, a useful description not only of the meetings he was to attend and the officials who were to be at them, but even of the issues that might be raised and what the background of those issues was. He said, 'Thank you, most helpful,' in a minimizing way, but it was clear to him that the paper was invaluable, and he felt that this was also clear to Miss Graine. He laid it casually to one side.

She now indicated the pile of documents which had been left for study, and which he had not touched. 'Shall I go through these for you?'

Pylos looked up. 'But shouldn't I –' he began, and then began again, 'It was felt by Mr Choudhury and Mr Chai . . .'

Miss Graine dismissed Choudhury and Chai with a slight

grimace which, while improper, contrasted flatteringly with her deferential attitude to Pylos. 'They mustn't bother you with trivialities.' She took away the Organization's Founding Constitution. 'I can mark passages for your attention, if you wish.' She paused. 'Of course, if you prefer . . .'

'No, that will be quite all right.' Pylos could not help being pleased to find his time was precious. 'Most helpful,' he said again, this time with irrepressible sincerity.

Miss Graine gave him one of her brief, pin-pointing smiles. 'I'll do it immediately.' She took the pile of documents and left the room.

When the weighted door had given its ultimate sealing click, Pylos placed the list of meetings before him. The fact that Sadie Graine had proved efficient in no way lightened his spirits – on the contrary, it oppressed him with disproportionate foreboding. He felt that her derogatory reference to Choudhury and Chai should not have been allowed to pass. But then, she really had not made any remark about them – and were they not, in truth, a rather Rosencrantz-and-Guildenstern pair? In any case, Pylos thought, pulling himself together, it's all absurd. She won't be here more than a few days. Appeased by this thought, he took up Miss Graine's useful list, leant back in his Organization chair, and began to study it.

Recounting the day to his wife that evening he mentioned Sadie Graine. 'What a secretary they've given me,' he said. 'A real battle-axe. But I'm going to ask for a change tomorrow.'

There followed some weeks of what Pylos was later to think of as the Phony War. As he made his first steps across the Organizational scene, Miss Graine was ever at his side and, although he could not relish the proximity, Pylos admitted to himself that she was worth her weight in gold. He now told himself that he would retain her merely for these weeks of settling-in. Disturbingly, he felt that Miss Graine herself sensed this callous intention – but perhaps this was imagination. Considering how much he had to cope with at this time, it was odd the way Sadie Graine preyed on his mind.

Pylos's first official act was to name his new department. The interim titles that had been used – 'Economic Relief of Under-Privileged Territories' and 'Mission for Under-Developed Lands' – were well enough in their way, but they combined a note of condescension with initials which, when contracted, proved somewhat unfortunate. Pylos consulted with senior members of the Designation and Terminology Branch, seeking some descriptive but trenchant phrase, some phrase that would neither patronize nor minimize. No agreement was reached until Miss Graine, clearing his tray one afternoon, offered her suggestion. So it was that DALTO came into being – the Department of Aid to the Less Technically Oriented.

Nevertheless, Pylos intended to rid himself of Miss Sadie Graine. It was the case of Ashmole-Brown that brought matters to a head.

In creating the staff of this new department, heads of existing departments had been asked to nominate those staff members in their ranks most fitted to initiate a programme of aid to the world's less-privileged. Many departments having naturally recommended those they could no longer tolerate themselves, a strangely assorted (and not wholly unsympathetic) crew was gradually assembled on a hitherto-unused floor of the building, and as DALTO reached its full complement of personnel, the remainder of the Organization's staff were able to close their expurgated ranks with a sigh of relief.

It was from this background that there advanced upon Achilles Pylos, a few weeks after his arrival at the Organization, the case of Ashmole-Brown.

Until he was assigned to the new department, Ashmole-Brown had been working away at his cluttered desk in the Department of Social and Anthropological Questions. Within a matter not of weeks but of days after the formation of DALTO, the contents of that small office, including Ashmole-Brown, had been completely transferred to the freshly partitioned premises three floors below. His papers were rushed through by hand, an unusual circumstance which in itself would have denoted emergency. To Ashmole-Brown it made not the slightest difference whether he was on the thirty-first or the twenty-eighth floor: his work was everything to him, and he pushed on with it, oblivious of change, his head bent to his swelling manuscript, his hand moving evenly from line to line. He was to be seen on his way to the Organization library, a closely written list in his hand; or returning, his head already lowered as if in anticipation of the next page, each arm bowed with a load of the heavy books so soon to be exchanged for others. His desk, his window-ledge, his bookshelves, even his grey-tiled floor, were piled with flagged volumes and curling documents. Whatever else Ashmole-Brown might be, he was no slacker: there could be no doubt that he was hard at it.

Hard at what? This was the question that had so perplexed the Social and Anthropological officials and, the answer eluding them, had finally resulted in the frenzied transfer of Ashmole-Brown to DALTO. Ashmole-Brown had been hired, long ago, to undertake a study – that much was certain. But why? And by whom? He had a contract in which the nature of the study was defined at length, and its terms of reference by no means precluded the incorporation of Ashmole-Brown in DALTO: they would scarcely have prevented his inclusion in any public institution, so liberally studded were they with the many-faceted gems of the sociological lexicon. Even to the most experienced decodifiers, the central message of this contract seemed indecipherable. Ashmole-Brown alone was certain of his task.

And did Ashmole-Brown then refuse to divulge the theme of his labours? Far from it. He liked nothing better. Jovially, he would seat the inquirer (and at first there had been a succession of these, some of them officially propelled) on his single extra chair – depositing the displaced pile of books onto the floor – and explain by the hour. He would show references to illustrate points, or drag out, from under a teetering stack, some document or article he had found invaluable. It all seemed to hang together at the time – the visitor would find himself murmuring, 'Most interesting' and even 'Fascinating' – but no one had yet emerged from such an interview with a coherent tale to tell. Ashmole-Brown's presence became a public confession of failure – a living expression of what his colleagues in Social and Anthropological Questions called the inability to communicate. Was he not using up official time and space? Was his rounded back in its antiquated tweeds not turned to two potentially useful windows? Might not the fluorescent light that shone down on him have shone more profitably on another? The Social and Anthropological Department, as a group, had experienced a meaningful, rewarding, and fully integrated sense of release when Ashmole-Brown was shunted off to DALTO.

One thing, however, had been overlooked. Ashmole-Brown's contract – his famous contract – contained a renewal clause. The contract in its present form had but short time to run, and the question of its renewal was presently brought to Mr Pylos's attention by Miss Sadie Graine.

Pylos was busy with affairs of the less technically oriented when Miss Graine came in with Ashmole-Brown's file. He waited for her to lay the papers on his In-tray and depart, but when she stood expectantly by the desk he knew that it was some matter to which she attached importance. Raising his head – not without some intrepid show of irritation – he invited, and received, the history of Ashmole-Brown. Miss Graine was at this time becoming more vocal, and she left no doubt as to the correct course to be followed. She would not, she explained, have bothered Pylos with the case had it not been for the rank of Ashmole-Brown. This – as Pylos saw from the cover of the file – though temporary, was substantial.

Alone again, Pylos laid aside the less technical and examined the dossier. The Organization kept two sets of files on its personnel. One of these recorded the halting progress of the staff member on his Organizational journey and, as has been noted, was uncompromisingly official in character: this was known as the Personal File. The other, known as the Confidential File, contained only personal details and was available to an authorized few. (Nothing can describe the repugnance felt by the staff for the existence of these Confidential dossiers. They believed, not unreasonably, that secret files could only contain facts, or fictions, that exposed or defamed them, and the knowledge that an extensive system was devoted to the accumulation of such records caused distress of a natural and well-founded kind.)

Pylos found that he had been given both files on Ashmole-Brown, bound together with a rubber band. Neither was large, and few minutes were required to read them. Ashmole-Brown had come in with the century, had been educated at a college in the north of England, where he had written a thesis on the legend of Perceforest, and had since been employed at universities and in the government. During the war he had spent some time in the Royal Navy until invalided out for allergies. He had served on government committees. His hobby seemed to be linguistics, and his single publication was a pamphlet entitled 'The Abuse of the Superlative in North America'. The only damaging item was a letter, in the Confidential file, in which a department store asked the Organization's assistance in obtaining payment of a small account one year overdue.

Ashmole-Brown was respectable. But was he respectable enough to stand up for? – to stand up for (though Pylos did not say it, even to himself) against Miss Sadie Graine? What if Ashmole-Brown should be around for years, a perpetual testimony to Pylos's administrative naïveté? If the name of Oxford or Cambridge had appeared in the file, Pylos would have taken heart on behalf of Ashmole-Brown. But Ashmole-Brown was not endorsed by either of these infallible bodies: his background was unmistakably redbrick in texture, and Pylos wavered.

It is not usual in the Organization for a department head to visit the offices of his staff. On taking up his appointment, Pylos had made an inaugural progress through his little domain, attended by Chai and Choudhury, and by his Chief of Missions, Rodriguez-O'Hearn. He had genially shaken hands and asked unexacting questions. He had stopped to chat with a filing clerk here, a secretary there; had spoken Greek with a Greek, and French with a Congolese. The staff had stood around their hastily tidied desks, and all but the most disillusioned had smiled. Pylos had peered into a Chinese typewriter and worked a Fotofax machine. He had admired the magnificent views from windows and refrained from commenting on the gloom of the windowless areas, which were more extensive. Within half an hour he had been safely back in his own room, his duty done. Since then, he had attended a departmental party, and made a token appearance in the staff cafeteria. What more could possibly have been asked?

The Chief Coordinator's decision to call on Ashmole-Brown was therefore a departure. Even Miss Graine looked startled, although she at once picked up her telephone and confirmed that Ashmole-Brown was in his cubicle at the far end of the corridor. Scattering a trio of gossiping girls, bringing alarmed heads up from drinking fountains as their owners prepared for flight, Pylos strode forth. Ultimately entering a labyrinth of partitions, he was shown into a narrow room by a wide-eyed secretary.

The only person who did not seem surprised was Ashmole-Brown.

Ashmole-Brown went through his usual chair-clearing process and, when Pylos was seated, settled himself back behind his desk. He was a broad, awkwardly-jointed man. His sagging tweeds and forward-flopping hair were of the same pepper-and-salt combination; even the round eyes shining out through the round lenses were densely speckled. The cheeks had retained their hectic schoolboy flush. The mouth was large, even generous, and presently said as if it meant it, 'Great pleasure to see you here, sir. Great pleasure.'

Pylos commented civilly on the evidence of Ashmole-Brown's industry, waving his hand towards the voluminous stacks – and in this way bringing one or two loose papers to the floor, where they were allowed to lie. He then said, with a serious levelling of voice, 'Mr Ashmole-Brown, I should like you to tell me something about your work.'

Ashmole-Brown beamed. 'Mr Pylos,' he said, 'I have worked – laboured, I may say – at this opus of mine for nearly four years, and I marvel, sir, I marvel, that today of all days you should choose to make this inquiry. I marvel.' He paused to do so. 'For today – this very morning – I reached a significant point in my journey. There is light, Mr Pylos – light at the end of the tunnel. The end of my pilgrimage is in sight.'

Pylos expanded with relief. 'I am delighted to hear it,' he said. 'That is, we all, I am sure –'

'Quite, quite.' Ashmole-Brown was radiant. He tilted back his chair. He took off his glasses and, holding them by the stems, twirled them round and round, allowing his eyes to sparkle unconfined.

'And how would you estimate the – ah – usefulness of your work?' Pylos inquired. 'At this stage.'

Ashmole-Brown pursed his lips reflectively. His glasses rotated more slowly between his fingers. 'It is sound,' he said judicially. 'Yes, I would say – it is sound.'

'Sound?' Pylos frowned. 'Not more than sound?'

'No more – yet no less. Sound, sir. Sound is the word I should choose.' There was silence while Ashmole-Brown politely declined to add another adjective. He broke into smiles again. 'The completed work, however, has become – if not a reality – no longer a myth. In another three years, I should say – yes, another three –'

'Three years *more*?'

'Give or take a few months, naturally. My path lies plain before me. There is, as I say, light: light at the –'

Here Ashmole-Brown gave an exultant twirl to his glasses and they spun out of his hands, hit the desk and fell to the floor. After a moment's surprise he dropped forward in his chair and fumbled short-sightedly on the floor around him. His speckled back heaved above the desk like the dorsal mound of some half-submerged sea-monster. Pylos could hear him breathing in short grunts. 'Now, where the devil . . . Ah, yes, yes, here we are.' Ashmole-Brown hove into sight once more, pinker in the face, holding the glasses in his hand. Pylos saw that one of the lenses was completely shattered.

Ashmole-Brown stared at the glasses for some moments. He then laid them on the desk before him. He seemed to have forgotten that Pylos was there. He shook his head heavily. 'This', he said, apparently to himself, 'will slow me down considerably.'

Pylos stirred in his chair, and Ashmole-Brown gave him a nod of recognition. He took up his glasses again and prodded the shattered side despondently with his forefinger. 'O piteous spectacle,' he declaimed. He then held the unbroken side vertically to his eye like a lorgnette and, after squinting through it at Pylos, lifted a half-completed page from the desk and attempted to read. His lips slowly formed the words as he identified them. He put the glasses down, seeming relieved. 'Dare say I can go on like that for a while,' he said.

'But surely,' Pylos exclaimed, aghast, 'they can be repaired in a matter of a day or two.'

Ashmole-Brown stared. 'My dear chap, no sense in that. No sense at all. I'm going on home leave in a few weeks. In England I can get a brand-new pair for nothing.'

After the dismissal of Ashmole-Brown, Pylos felt himself to be full-fledged. It was as if he had passed through some ceremony of Organizational initiation, forged some invisible bond with his fellow administrators. He now settled in to his coordinational duties in earnest. With Miss Graine's assistance, a pattern was formed – one he was to follow for years, a routine of discussions, decisions and correspondence which his position invested with parochial grandeur.

During the process of establishment, Miss Graine proved indispensable – so much so that Pylos eventually relinquished all intention of dispensing with her, and even forgot that he had wished to. A man like Pylos, between whose abilities and whose position there lie certain gaps, needs a woman like Miss Sadie Graine. For Miss Graine made it her business to plug those gaps – with flattery of Pylos, with disparagement of his equals, with inequities to his underlings, with whatever unsightly wadding came to hand. It was her daily task to fortify the dikes of Pylos's self-esteem. The excessive credence he put in her high opinion of himself soon naturally extended to her other views. He came to accept her judgements, and these judgements gradually took on a note of instruction.

For Miss Graine, too, the incident of Ashmole-Brown had

been significant. After that she became steadily more vocal, more peremptory. Silence lends stature, and Miss Graine, growing talkative, revealed herself to her colleagues as petty and acrimonious. She condemned unthinkingly, and was open to no rational explanation. (She had a curious habit of saying 'I'll admit that,' 'I grant that,' 'I'll say that much,' as if acknowledging that any reasonable admission must be forced out of her.) She quickly made her new power felt, letting it be known that she had instigated the fatal investigation of Ashmole-Brown, and becoming feared as a result. A few tried, with fleeting success, to ingratiate themselves with her; most merely sought to keep out of her way, saying they would not go against The Graine. Keeping out of her way was not easy. She set up in her office an intricate system of files covering the activities of the department, so that Pylos might have immediate access to them. These files were methodically kept: though it were method, however, there was madness in it – or at least obsession, for they duplicated, from various angles, other records kept elsewhere. No one dared to point this out. She also miraculously retained in her head, keeping it otherwise vacant for the purpose, all manner of statistics referring to the less technically oriented as well as to the DALTO personnel.

In assessing Miss Graine's character, her single status was taken into account – inevitably, but perhaps excessively. For had Miss Graine ever been seriously contemplated as a life partner, had she even been asked – let alone taken – in marriage, her demands on the world might have been different.

Senior members of Pylos's staff would compliment him on her efficiency, saying 'What would you do without her?' As time wore on, a note of wistful speculation crept into this rhetorical inquiry, and it developed the ring of a real question. There was, indeed, no way of knowing what his stature at the Organization might have been, had he fallen under some other influence than that of Sadie Graine. As it was, he came to feel pleasantly important as he trod the Organization's lobbies or rode its elevators. His dark, portly good looks were recognizable, and he was greeted wherever he went. He gradually formed a circle of acquaintances; not precisely intimates, these were more in the nature of cronies – their talk did not extend beyond shop, but this shop was sometimes talked in their living-rooms as well as their offices. Although exalted in Organizational rank, they were not remarkable men. First-class minds, being interested in the truth, tend to select other first-class minds as companions. Second-class minds, on the other hand, being interested in themselves, will select third-class comrades in order to maintain an illusion of superiority; and it was this way with Pylos.

A lingering adroitness saved him from utter mediocrity, and it was this adroitness, together with the promptings of Miss Sadie Graine, that helped him sense the temper of the Organization and dictated the tone of his dealings with his staff.

There was, for example, his masterly handling of Choudhury's request for promotion. Although this came soon after the Ashmole-Brown episode, Pylos was already acting with more assurance. When Miss Graine, with lips meaningly tightened, admitted Choudhury to his office, Pylos was prepared. And when Choudhury, with unprecedented eloquence, pleaded his case, Pylos made no outward resistance. As it happened, he had just come from a top-level meeting at which the Director-General of the Organization had enjoined his departmental chiefs to administrative stringency, due to a crisis in Organization funds. Pylos could conceivably have given Choudhury this straightforward and authentic reason for refusal; the fact that he did not shows the velocity with which Pylos was learning the Organizational ropes. He did tell Choudhury that he had discussed the matter of promotions with the Director-General that very morning. The Director-General, he went on, put a certain emphasis on seniority. Years of service, years of experience – age, in short – mattered to him, perhaps more than they did to . . . (here Pylos gave a rueful, self-indicating smile) . . . others. Choudhury, for all his outstanding ability, was a comparatively young man. Could he not be patient? At his age, a matter of two or three years – what were they? Could he not take them in his youthful stride? So Pylos appealed, and Choudhury submitted.

Yes, Mr Pylos had an appealing manner, and he used it for that purpose. He aimed to please, and his aim was directed to the highest circles. After a while he developed a posture that had always been latent with him – an excessively upright posture verging on a strut. He walked as if he were bending over backwards.

Miss Graine's responsibilities having increased, she was provided with the help of a typist, who was accommodated in an inside office that had been – and continued to be – used for hats and coats. The makeshift setting was well-suited – and perhaps contributed – to the constant turnover of the girls engaged. One of these girls, it is true, made an attempt to relate the story of Miss Sadie Graine to the Department of Personnel during the third year of Mr Pylos's administration. The tale, told with earnest lucidity, moved her hearer – a personnel officer of mature years and large bun – to send subsequently for the Confidential file on Miss Graine. But on finding this to be a veritable treasure-house of testimonials lavishly endorsed by the upper echelons of DALTO, she returned it unmarked to the registry and requested in its place the file on the typist – in which she entered a brief account of the typist's appeal, adding a notation with respect to paranoid tendencies. Shortly afterwards the girl was sent to assist the less technical in rugged country northwest of Kabul.

The environs of Kabul were not the only locality to benefit in this way. Those who served the Organization in DALTO projects throughout the world soon began to give an impression of being divided into two groups: those who had volunteered for such service, and those who had displeased Miss Sadie Graine. The senior officers of Pylos's staff were dedicated men; in order to conserve their efforts the more completely for the far-flung needy of the world, they took the precaution of doing nothing for those close to them. One or two who fell below this lofty standard and intervened on behalf of their subordinates were quickly eliminated by Miss Graine.

Of the more junior staff, some – and particularly those who foresaw a sojourn in Kabul – condemned Pylos. Others, of larger nature, contended that he was a weak man but a man of goodwill. Whatever their view, not a day passed without their taking some stock of the situation. Over their typewriters, over their desks, over their morning coffee, over a period of five years, the staff of Pylos recounted to one another, week in, week out, successive chapters in the tale of Sadie Graine.

With regard to the less technically oriented, all the efforts of Miss Graine were required to shield Pylos from troublesome ambiguities. He sincerely wished to assist the laggard lands commended to his care. Yet he looked about him at the fully oriented, and in his heart he wondered. Was this the state of mind one sought to purvey to the less privileged? It was true that the grievous condition of many of the countries assisted by DALTO seemed to justify almost anything that was done to them – providing, as it were, a mandate for any change, the bad along with the good. About this development process there appeared to be no half-measures: once a country had admitted its backwardness, it could hope for no quarter in the matter of improvement. It could not accept a box of pills without accepting, in principle, an atomic reactor. Progress was a draught that must be drained to the last bitter drop.

Once, after a day-long conference on Civic Coordination projects, it occurred to Pylos that progress might have taken different, unimagined forms; but he soon dismissed this idea for what it was, the result of mental strain. Occasionally he wondered if more thought might not have been given to the ultimate consequences of technical change – change about which, indeed, the word 'impact' was frequently used. More thought – but by whom? Not by Pylos. Pylos was intent on staying on top of things, not getting to the bottom of them. If there was one thing Pylos didn't go for it was being asked to consider complexities at any length and for their own sake. He could turn quite nasty if pressed to do so.

Achilles Pylos could only hope that the backward nations, once technically oriented, would make some happier use of this condition than their mentors had.

He found himself obliged to participate in what were called far-reaching decisions concerning countries of whose language he was ignorant, whose customs he had never studied, whose religion was a puzzle to him, whose politics a labyrinth, whose history a mystery. For this purpose he was provided with advisers whose qualifications did not in every instance exceed his own capacities – and with documents whose abundance invariably did. And at intervals he made headlong journeys to inspect the work of DALTO around the world.

When in this way he visited DALTO projects in the field – to gain, as the saying goes, first-hand knowledge – he was generally received in spacious offices and whisked about, to institutes and farms, to factories and dam-sites, in large cars. He stayed in air-conditioned hotels and was entertained in important houses. He could not quite convince himself that this led to first-hand knowledge. But since he did not believe in useless suffering he was also displeased when he came upon a DALTO mission existing without such amenities, and would depart promising to rectify the situation.

These contradictions caused him dismay, but Pylos suppressed his misgivings, with the help of Sadie Graine – who urged upon him matters of more immediate importance, such as jurisdictional disputes with fellow aid-agencies over specific rights to assist the needy. Any important deviation from established Organization practices would have necessitated a character very different from his. Faintly he trusted to the larger hope – that something less than ill would be the final goal of good. Sometimes he consoled himself with the simple fact that he, one of DALTO's own officers, was aware of such inconsistencies. This seemed to help somewhat.

On the fifth anniversary of Pylos's arrival at the Organization, a new leaf, turned by an unexpected hand, was opened in the story of Miss Sadie Graine.

That evening, for the first time, Sadie Graine came to dinner at the Pylos apartment. Mrs Pylos had often spoken with Miss Graine on the telephone, and had glimpsed her occasionally in her husband's office. Once in a while she had said to Pylos, 'Shouldn't we ask your secretary to dinner?' Pylos, from some instinct which he could not then explain but which was later vindicated, had repeatedly turned the suggestion aside. At last the anniversary celebration presented itself, and Mrs Pylos, saying 'Achilles, don't be ridiculous,' had telephoned Miss Graine and invited her to dinner.

The evening seemed to go well enough. There were several other guests, and along the table Pylos saw his wife talking in her usual charming way with Miss Sadie Graine. He even heard her say, 'Do call me Ismene.' It was unnecessary, even indecent, to contrast his wife, with her elegant golden head and great grey eyes, with Sadie Graine, with her tight little lips and tight little dark blue dress; but Pylos was touched to observe that Sadie Graine had a new permanent wave for the occasion.

When the guests had gone – and, being official guests, they left early – Mrs Pylos put her feet up on the sofa while her husband went around opening windows and replacing a chair or two. They remarked how So-and-So had put on weight, how his wife had been wearing a wig, how someone else had been allergic to the mousse. And at last the conversation reached Miss Sadie Graine.

'Really darling,' said Mrs Pylos, taking off her bracelet and laying it on the coffee-table beside her. 'What an *ἀπολειφάδι*.'

Pylos was startled. His wife was a kind woman – in fact, as beautiful women go, a very kind woman. It was not her habit to take strong dislikes or to use strong language. He opened a window he had just closed. 'How is that, my dear?'

'I should have thought', his wife went on, 'that you might just as well have kept the first one.'

Pylos now came and sat down. 'Ismene, I don't understand you at all. What first one?'

'Why Achilles, don't you remember? When you first joined the Organization they gave you an impossible secretary – some nasty old thing, you told me – and you sent her away and asked for a different one. Now, don't tell me you've forgotten. All I'm saying is – she couldn't have been much worse than this one.'

Pylos lit a cigarette. He looked so concerned that his wife concluded he must be thinking of something else. Eventually he said, however, 'I suppose it does come to much the same thing.'

*

The following morning, Choudhury had an early appointment to see Pylos. The two men sat down together, freshly shaven and smelling faintly of cologne, in Pylos's office. The morning light was particularly brilliant, and Pylos was taken aback to notice a change in Choudhury. Choudhury was looking seedy. His eyes were circled, his cheeks sunken, his black hair coarsely threaded with white. Pylos realized that, although he saw Choudhury almost daily, he had not really looked at him for some time. Ah well, he told himself, we're all getting on, I suppose, and there's nothing we can do about it. 'How are you getting on, Yussuf?' he inquired pleasantly. 'And what can I do for you?'

'Mr Pylos,' said Choudhury, leaning forward in his chair and putting his hand earnestly on the edge of the desk, 'you may remember that I once spoke to you about my promotion.'

Pylos responded, 'Of course' – not because he remembered at all, but because it really *was* a matter of course: it seemed to Pylos that scarcely a day passed without some member of his staff raising the question of their promotion, and there was no reason why Choudhury should have been an exception. Like most department heads at the Organization he had come to regard these petitioners as neurotic nuisances – and in fact by the time they reached Pylos they were often acting pretty queerly. In each case he received the applicant with a sense of long-suffering, even of martyrdom.

'I know you have a lot on your mind,' Choudhury went on, 'and I haven't bothered you again until now. I kept hoping that something would develop. But I wonder – it's been so long – can you tell me how my case stands?'

Pylos saw that he would have to deal more or less frankly with Choudhury. The Director-General was at that moment discouraging promotions – due to a severe financial crisis – and the prospects of advancement for someone like Choudhury were distant indeed. Pylos leant his elbows on the desk and brought the tips of his fingers together. He looked hard at Choudhury, and it struck him again how worn Choudhury was looking. Taking his cue from Choudhury's appearance, he spoke.

'Yussuf,' he said, 'as you know, we now have a new Director-General – a younger man, a man of great energy and – I say it in no pejorative sense – ambition. He has made it known that he will want the upper positions of the Organization to be filled increasingly by men and women of youth and vigour like himself. Naturally, he respects the abilities – I may say, the devotion – of' (here Pylos gave a rueful smile) 'old-stagers like ourselves. But I would be less than honest with you if I did not mention that this new emphasis on a younger staff may hamper your prospects for the immediate future.'

As Pylos uttered these words and leant back in his chair, not displeased with himself, Choudhury's hands convulsively grasped the edge of the desk, and Choudhury himself turned grey. He got to his feet and, still gripping the edge of the desk as if he would tip it over, uttered a stream of agitated words in his own language. Pylos, greatly shocked, remained seated with an effort, looking up into Choudhury's wild eyes. Such a thing had never happened to him before, and fortunately it did not last long. In a moment or two Choudhury subsided, and sank down trembling into his chair. His breath came and went sobbingly; his forehead was wet, his hands quivered. He murmured a distraught apology.

Maintaining a certain reserve, Pylos reassured him. 'You must have been over-working,' he said. 'Letting things get you down.'

But Choudhury, doubtless not wishing to compound the impression of decrepitude, denied this. Limply he asked leave to go. Pylos saw him to the door. He put his hand on Choudhury's arm. 'We'll have to see what can be done about your future,' he said – his thoughts already turning towards Kabul.

When Choudhury had gone, Pylos sat down again. He wanted to forget what had just taken place, but he could not face the contents of his In-tray so he simply sat there for a while, feeling uneasy. It wasn't so much Choudhury's going to pieces that bothered him: it was what Choudhury had said. Not that Pylos understood a word of Urdu, of course. But he knew well enough when he heard the name of Sadie Graine.

Once in a great while, it happens that a scholarly book, a large, difficult and demanding book, a book not devoid of footnotes and statistics, will by its very erudition engage the public interest. It was so with Gibbon's first volume; it has happened more recently with the respective works of Professor Myrdal and Doctor Kinsey. And thus it was with the work of Ashmole-Brown.

The Organization had forgotten Ashmole-Brown. Five years earlier, Ashmole-Brown had been handed his final pay-cheque, an envelope containing his travel authorization and steamer-tickets, and a receipt for his relinquished *laissez-passer*. He had got into the Down elevator and gone out through the Organization's revolving doors, and there had been no reason to think of Ashmole-Brown ever again. Ashmole-Brown had been terminated. What, then, was Ashmole-Brown doing on the inside page of the morning newspaper, grinning broadly as he stepped ashore on the very pier from which he had been summarily dispatched? According to the legend beneath the photograph, he was arriving for the publication of his book *Candle of Understanding*, which had recently created a sensation in England.

The photograph was indistinct, the legend brief. But it was Ashmole-Brown all right. The same eyes beamed through (intact) spectacles, the same shaggy tweeds were furled around ungainly limbs. Those at the Organization who saw the photograph were subtly troubled by this breakdown in the natural order of things. It was as if an old film had been run through the projector in reverse, and Ashmole-Brown were seen descending instead of mounting the gang-way of his out-bound vessel. It gave them a sense of witnessing some act of prodigious insubordination.

A few days later, glancing through a picture-magazine in the Organization barber-shop, Pylos came upon the same photograph of Ashmole-Brown – this time, large, sharp and glossy and followed by several others. 'Great to be back,' Ashmole-Brown was quoted – somewhat improbably – as having said. The caption proceeded to explain that he had been to these shores before and that he had at one time worked for the Organization. In a brief interview on the facing page, Ashmole-Brown was reported as having, among other things, modestly brushed aside the assumption that he had resigned from the Organization in order to devote himself exclusively to the completion of his great work. 'Resigned? Not a bit of it,' he exclaimed (with, so it was recounted, a genial guffaw). 'Dismissed, more like it. Turfed out. Jolly well turfed out.' No particular importance was attached to this revelation, and the sequence of photographs went on to depict a series of genial guffaws.

During the weeks that followed, Pylos saw much of Ashmole-Brown. His guffaw, along with innumerable copies of his immense and expensive book, was to be seen in bookshop windows, in railway carriages and on coffee-tables. *Candle of Understanding* was advertised, lyrically and at length, in newspapers which also reviewed it with no less lyricism and no greater brevity. It was praised by specialists and laymen alike. One learnt that Ashmole-Brown was lecturing to various august assemblies, and that he would discuss his book late at night on a television programme called 'Last Gasp'. Finally Pylos came home one evening to find the book in his own living-room. The next day he took it with him to the office.

There he placed the book before him on his desk and examined its black and white jacket. 'A Study in Technology and Humanism' was printed below the title. From the front flap Pylos learnt that Ashmole-Brown had spent eight years compiling this examination of what was called 'the diverse traditions, merging present and common destiny of men'. Ashmole-Brown, so the paragraph said, had concerned himself with the historical and current effects of technical change on indigenous cultures; had based himself on the ingenious premise that there was something to be learnt from the sum of human experience. There followed a brief summary of the author's background, with a mention of his four years at the Organization. Ashmole-Brown was married, had a grown daughter, and cultivated his garden near Colchester. Pylos turned the preliminary pages and began Chapter I.

Half an hour later he closed the book and laid his hand upon it. Between his fingers the jacket interjected 'Literate' and 'Illuminating'. He could not deny it. Ashmole-Brown had obviously written an extraordinary book. Here were the contradictions which Pylos had failed to confront during his years with the less technically oriented. Here – but presented with what sympathy, what grace, what goodwill, and yet with what authority – were just such insights as Pylos would have wished to have; just such solutions as he would have wished to propose. It was undeniable: the book was masterly.

There was something grotesque, even terrifying, about the idea that Ashmole-Brown's great work had all this while been accreting, like an iceberg, for the good ship Pylos to founder upon. Pylos groaned, and opened the back flap of the jacket.

From this he learnt that Ashmole-Brown had taken his

title from the Apocrypha. Well, why not? Was not Ashmole-Brown himself out of the Apocrypha, in a manner of speaking? But why the devil had the man not said his work was this important? 'Sound,' he had said; Pylos could just see him saying it: 'I should call it sound.' Did he not realize that no one talked like that these days? One did not minimize one's achievements – indeed, such diffidence was open to damaging psychological interpretations. It wasn't done. And yet – Ashmole-Brown was exactly the type who would do it, and Pylos felt he should have known. Damn the man, had he not even written some pamphlet – now it all came back to Pylos – yes, a pamphlet on the abuse of the superlative? (This work appeared in paperback shortly afterwards and, advertised as 'Early Ashmole-Brown', sold extensively.) Pylos groaned again, and he turned the book over on its face. From the back cover, Ashmole-Brown's round face looked up at him, creased for a mild guffaw.

Pylos was a man who could recognize his own defects. He could not, however, dwell on them. Tracing the Ashmole-Brown débâcle back to its origins, he swiftly recalled that he had been new to the Organization at the time, and that Ashmole-Brown had been virtually unknown to him. Soon he was reproaching himself for nothing more than having relied too heavily on the judgement of others. And these others were quickly fused into a single figure.

Miss Graine, seeing Ashmole-Brown's book on Pylos's desk, had experienced a feeling of dread. It was not simply the existence of the book; it was the fact of Pylos's having left it there, in flagrant violation of their mutual security pact. The sensation that her power was passing communicated itself, mysteriously, from Miss Graine to her colleagues. Exhibiting a new sense of impunity, several people drew her attention to articles on Ashmole-Brown, ingenuously asking if she remembered him. One morning she found a magazine on her desk, opened to a large heading: 'Are You an Ashmole-Brown Enthusiast?'

The Ashmole-Brown development was in fact causing unrest throughout DALTO. The sooner his candle of understanding guttered out, the better it would be all round, and especially for Pylos. But Ashmole-Brown's success gave no sign of flagging. The fact that no official recognition had been forthcoming for this exceptional case was encouraging a sense of injustice in all – where a juster system would have imposed proportionate expectations. The staff, though naturally enjoying the discomfiture of authority, felt that the joke was somehow on them. Some token acknowledgement of their dissatisfaction was called for.

It happened that Miss Graine, passing by the Organization bar one day on her way back from lunch, glimpsed Mr Pylos in earnest conversation with one of his friends – another Greek, named Apostolides, who had recently become head of the section dealing with staff assignments abroad. Now there were a hundred official matters that Pylos might have earnestly discussed with Apostolides, and there was no reason why Miss Graine should have been alarmed by the sight of the two together. Nevertheless it is true that all the way back to her office she was haunted by a quotation that she could neither place nor complete: 'When Greek meets Greek,' she repeated to herself, and wondered what came next. If she had ever known, she could not remember. But she felt sure it was nothing good.

When Sadie Graine was assigned to Central America, she appealed against the decision. She contested it on the grounds that she did not speak the language – a not unreasonable objection but one which had not operated on behalf of those still labouring in localities like Kabul. Her objection was over-ridden and her assignment confirmed for a period of two years, with possibility of extension.

It will be thought that Miss Sadie Graine got what she asked for. But who, surveying the course of his own life, can honestly say that he has not asked for something he yet hoped not to get?

It only remained to choose a farewell present for Miss Graine and give her a departmental party. Pylos, when asked for his advice regarding the gift, suggested a suitcase. The idea was proposed to the subscribing staff members, and met with such enthusiastic response that a set of Spanish language records was bought with the money left over.

There had been many farewell parties in DALTO since its inception, but none so well attended as the one given for Miss Graine. It was held at the end of the day, in a private room adjoining the Disarmament Council lounge. Drinks were served, with nuts and potato chips, and the merriment seemed at times almost saturnalian. When gaiety began to verge on rowdiness, Choudhury – who was looking particularly fit – called for silence, and Pylos made a short speech. It was a speech similar to many he had given before, expressing fervent appreciation for Miss Graine's services, profound regret at her departure, and great pride that she had been selected for this difficult mission. He dwelt, with some office pleasantries, upon his own self-sacrifice, depicting himself as a man willing to renounce his own well-being for the greater good: Mr Pylos, in effect, had loved not Caesar less, but Rome more. The response to his jokes was overwhelming, the ultimate applause deafening. The suitcase, and a box of records labelled 'Never Too Late to Learn', were brought forward. So was Miss Sadie Graine. Pylos made the presentation, calling her Sadie for the first time.

He had intended to kiss her on both cheeks, but could only rise to one when the moment came.

6. Official Life

'Tuesdays are the worst,' Luba said. She was sitting on a chair in Ismet's office taking off her waterproof boots. A succession of people had used the chair for the same purpose in the last fifteen minutes because the office coat-rack was just outside Ismet's door. This annoyed Ismet in general, and he minded particularly when it was Luba.

Luba, a beauty, was looking terrible – her auburn hair newly released from a plastic headdress but soaking all the same, her open coat revealing a succession of sweaters, her sleep-flattened face not made up. 'Tuesday mornings are worse than Mondays, I tell you why. Mondays you're still fresh from the week-end. Wednesday you already look forward to Friday. But Tuesdays – Ismet, I tell you, Tuesdays are No Man's Land.' Now she had her boots off but still sat on the edge of the chair, holding each boot up by its top. Her accent thickened when she got emotional, which was a good deal of the time. 'What a morning. An hour to get here. What a country.' She rolled her eyes towards the grey window. 'Did you see the television last night? Not one thing worth seeing. I watched till midnight. I told my husband, What decadence.'

Go away, Ismet was saying, in his mind and his own language. Go away.

'What would I give to go away. Now the pension can be drawn at fifty-five, I count to myself, how many years. Still so many.' Luba put her hand to her lank hair and repeated quickly, 'So very many.'

'Jaspersen's going to the Committee this morning.' Ismet drew attention to the work on his desk. 'I have to prepare –'

'Jaspersen's going down? What's being discussed?'

'Item Six. The Question of Unification.' Ismet again pointed to the papers on his blotter. The Question of Unification came up annually. Countries had been divided, subdivided. Some pleaded to be put back, others demanded guarantees that it would never happen.

Ismet's phone rang. He snatched it up without looking to see if his secretary had arrived at her desk by the coat-rack. 'Contingency Section, Ismet.' Before anyone spoke, he gave Luba an apologetic nod over the mouthpiece, denoting a long conversation. 'Ah – Mr Nagashima, yes, I called you yesterday evening but you'd already gone. . . . No, no, of course, it was well after hours, I was working late and didn't keep track of the . . . Yes, the Question of Unification. I think you have a false docket from the main file.'

Luba stood up, still holding a boot in each hand. 'That Nagashima loses things,' she said. 'Once, a whole set of working-papers.'

Ismet said into the phone, 'When you find it, then, perhaps you'd call me.'

Luba nodded. 'Another time, a folder of MOVs.' These were Miscellaneous Obligating Vouchers.

'Let us lunch some time,' said Ismet, prolonging the telephone conversation in the hope that Luba would leave. 'Yes. Thursday would be fine.' He turned the pages of his desk calendar with his left hand and found the day blank. However, since Luba now did leave, he said into the phone, 'Sorry, I do have something – another day perhaps. Let's be in touch when you find the file then.' He replaced the receiver quietly and lifted the uppermost folder from his tray.

A shadow on the frosted-glass partition alongside his open door informed him that Leslie, his secretary, had arrived. Not wishing to advertise her lateness, she alone of all the section did not use his chair to take off her boots.

'Leslie,' he called.

There was a scuffle and a suppressed metallic scraping as

she hung up her coat, then Leslie appeared. Leslie had shoulder-length brown hair and darkly outlined eyes. Her stockings, yesterday of black wool, were of white lattice today. She said truculently, 'I'm sorry.' She was new to the section and had not quite established her right to address Ismet by his first name, although she invariably used it behind his back. Since he was only Step Two in the Specialized Category, she disdained to address him formally. 'This rain,' she said. 'Pee-*ew*!'

Ismet could not get up the nerve to admonish her after all. He said, 'I'm preparing a paper. I don't want to be disturbed unless it's urgent. Do you have something to go on with?'

'I'm collating.'

'How long will that take you?'

Leslie made an estimate, doubled it. 'Half an hour.'

Ismet added to his many defeats by letting her go. At her desk outside he heard her take up the phone and dial her friend in the typing pool. Her husky voice was at its most pervasive when lowered. 'I went to this dance,' she said, 'the one on the bulletin board. Pee-*ew*!'

Ismet drew a typed sheet towards him. A memorandum – to, through, and from higher authorities, with copies to those higher still – had been sent to him for a draft reply. 'Pending accrual,' it began. Ismet bowed his head over his work.

Nagashima was standing by his window, watching the rain. These winter downpours were, to be sure, no worse than the spring rains of his own country, yet how he disliked them, what nostalgia he felt, leaning from this window of another world, looking on a scene that contained scarcely one familiar item. An immense building was being demolished nearby, the walls smashed by repeated blows of a swinging metal ball. An almost identical building would certainly rise from these smashes. In Japan, too, temples had been erected and re-erected on the same sites over centuries. Obviously a similar sense of continuity was involved, but he had not been able to link the two traditions.

He looked down at his window-sill – a broad inner ledge formed by the covers of the heating apparatus and, in Nagashima's case, completely stacked with dossiers, with folders, with innumerable, unmemorable documents. (Just yesterday he had been informed once more that it was forbidden to cover the heating vents in this way, but where then could these papers possibly go?) The false docket – such a strange name, like some treacherous Dutchman – that Ismet wanted was there, he knew, must be there, but he would never find it. He would lift them all, examine each title, his fingers would become frantic, his palms moist, but he would not find it. This had happened so often now that he sometimes did not look at all. The papers had ceased to be – had perhaps never been – quite real to him. If he actually believed in the existence of the file, then he might find it.

Once he had almost believed in these files and their dockets; had come, indeed, to the Organization as full of assiduity and goodwill as the refinements of his upbringing would allow. But his goodwill had glanced off the Organization like calf-love off a courtesan – the Organization did not require or even notice it. Unrequited, it had become a somewhat humiliating burden, furtively borne. Nagashima sighed, shifting but not unsettling this weight.

He began to turn over the first pile of folders. Ismet's file wouldn't be there – but here was the set of vouchers someone had wanted last month, that woman, also of Ismet's section, the one with the face like a cliff. Nagashima put the vouchers in an old inter-office envelope and sent them to Luba, having heavily scratched out his name on the envelope as former addressee.

'If I had high cheekbones like yours,' said a chubby little girl named Gabrielle, 'I'd do my hair like Greta Garbo.' She came to stand next to Luba at the mirror where she was making up her face. Through an oversight, the ladies' room had an inordinate share of windows, but the fluorescent tube over its mirrored counter gave a light so ghastly that it was rumoured to have been systematically chosen as the result of a time-and-motion study.

Luba, whose ability to admire her own image, however poorly illuminated, was a match for any time-and-motion study, went on applying rouge. She looked pleased. 'It is the planes,' she said.

Gabrielle looked towards the window. 'Planes?'

'The planes of the face.' Luba was growing rosier with every twirl of her fingers. 'Garbo has planes. I see her in the street. No make-up, old clothes, nothing fashionable. Only planes. She is the friend of a very close friend.'

'I can't use that.' Gabrielle was examining Luba's powder-box. 'I have it specially made. My skin is too sens –'

'Who's looking after the phones?' asked Luba abruptly. 'The phones must be covered. Time after time I say it. Time after time, every girl leaves his desk.'

Gabrielle said sulkily, 'Leslie's there.' At that moment Leslie came into the room, and Gabrielle went out without a word.

Leslie came to the mirror and whitened her lips a little with a lipstick taken from her pocket. She carried a small assortment of cosmetics in her pocket in order not to be seen leaving the office with her handbag. Over her ashen face she flicked a chalky puff. 'What do you use?' she asked, taking up Luba's powder-box.

Luba finished with her hair and took the powder-box back. 'I'm just using that up,' she said. 'It's not really right for me. My skin's too sensitive.' Seeing Leslie's sceptical look in the mirror, she added, 'Would you like it?'

Leslie said coolly, 'Jaspersen was looking for you.'

'What? Just now?' Luba began ramming objects into her handbag. 'Why didn't you tell me?' She met her own wild eyes in the glass. 'No time. Never any time.' She transferred her glance again to Leslie. 'No wonder we look as we do.'

'It's O.K.' Leslie brought out a bottle of iridescent nail lacquer from her pocket and began to shake it, her first vigorous action of the day. 'He's gone to the Committee now.'

Jaspersen took up his resolution – his draft resolution, that is to say, with its folder of proposed amendments – bent over his In-tray to read a note on the topmost file there, and walked across to the windows. Jaspersen's office was carpeted, an obvious indication of senior rank; the carpet was grey and somewhat worn – a more subtle suggestion, perhaps, of modifications within seniority. On Jaspersen's desk the density of paper was as great as on Nagashima's window-sill, but these papers of Jaspersen's – these files and false dockets, these drafts for approval and final versions for signature – gave an impression of having just alighted, or of forming the course of an ever-flowing stream, whereas Nagashima's were as still and stagnant as lake water.

Jaspersen was a man whose Out-tray was fuller than his In-tray; whose head was above water, whose feet were on the ground. Who administered a section, and would one day direct a branch. Jaspersen had everything to live for – in short, every reason to get up in the morning and come to his office. For years he had tranquilly pursued his work as head of the Contingency and Unresolved Disputes Section, and would eventually go on to even more gratifying tasks in areas yet more contentious.

Nevertheless, on this morning when the Question of Unification was coming up for debate, Jaspersen was in a melancholy mood. Although this was unusual for him, it had happened before, and he understood that the mood would pass away. Jaspersen had been heard to say that the Organization was his religion, and it is well known that moments of unaccountable doubt are the earmarks of the devout. Jaspersen had even gone so far as to make this analogy to himself. At such times he had learned to immerse himself more deeply than ever in his work, and with this in mind he now lifted two documents – the Provisional Report of the Working Group on Unforeseeable Contingencies, and a Study on the Harnessing of Cartographic Skills – from his window-sill and set them aside for reading at home that evening.

This mood of Jaspersen's would not even have been discernible beyond the Organization's walls. Had it been suggested, for instance, by some uninformed outsider, that the Organization had ever seriously erred in some particular, that it had ever acted with less than its potential effectuality, Jaspersen would have been as ready as always to correct this misconception with precise legal and statistical information; to cite chapter and verse – or, rather, resolution and amendment (while acknowledging, with wry witticisms, the larger but more bearable truth of universal human fallibility).

Jaspersen looked at his watch. It was now long past the hour set for the opening of the Committee meeting, and even a little past the time at which it might actually have begun. Jaspersen left his office, inquired for Luba of one of the secretaries, and, not finding her in, put his head around the door of his deputy, an Italian named Pastore.

Girolamo Pastore had been standing by the window. In fact, his window was directly below Nagashima's and, had the human eye been capable of distinguishing forms thirty storeys up, the two would have been on view in identical attitudes, one a few inches above the other and quite unaware of the proximity. Pastore's gaze travelled over buildings of glass, buildings of aluminium, a building with a sharp pinnacle that looked like a hypodermic needle stood on end. Why was it, Pastore was wondering, that at the very moment when architecture began to use the limitless upward resource of the sky ceilings had become so very low? More than commercialism: something to do with man's ceasing to demand noble rooms for himself, taking less pride in being a man. A man by himself – what was that these days? One counted merely as – a member of the staff.

In the Mediterranean town from which Pastore came, the streets were lined with small palaces whose every balcony invited the delivery of an oration (not that those balconies and their orators had proved entirely free from disadvantages); whose great doorways and windows offered glimpses of supreme moments in artistic creation; whose interiors gave on to courtyards adorned with fountains, with flowers, with curving stairs –

'You look as if you're delivering an oration.'

Pastore turned round. 'I was wondering whatever became of the *cortile*.'

Jaspersen frowned. 'The courtyard? I suppose it interfered with clean lines.'

Pastore looked gloomy. 'This clean-up campaign.' He put his hand to his breast. 'Western Man –'

How tiresome sometimes, thought Jaspersen, was Western Man with all his myths of Western Man. He interrupted. 'I'm going down to the Committee. Will you keep an eye on things here? Luba's disappeared.'

'I fear she can be traced.' Pastore waved his hand. 'Yes, yes, I'll be here.'

Jaspersen was thin and straight with long legs, and he walked quickly even when going only as far as the elevators. Besides, he preferred to make his way as rapidly as possible through his section's depressing inner corridor – airless, windowless, and painted grey – where a dozen typists leant woollen elbows on stained desks. Had there been some solution for these unfortunate conditions, Jaspersen, a humane man, would have proposed it. But he knew that nothing could be done – the designers of the building having judged such functional disadvantages to be small concessions made to outward harmony.

(The Organization had been founded at the end of a colossal world war – a moment when the spirit of international cooperation was naturally at its height. Scarcely had the Founding Constitution been signed by the participating nations when a commission of the world's foremost architects was formed to draw up plans for a building that would house this noble expression of human solidarity. The commission, in turn, had hardly sat to its task before certain fissures began to appear in the fabric of its deliberations: Dutchman contended with Swede, and Swede with Turk; Burmese fended off Brazilian, and Spaniard (through an interpreter) disparaged Swiss. The first to resign, a Frenchman who described his colleagues as being at loggerheads, subsequently became a recluse. The second, an elderly Belgian, was taken on a world cruise by his spinster niece and ultimately regained his health. The eventual design, endorsed by a group of three, was remarkable for its extensive use of conflicting primary forms, and was fittingly hailed throughout the world as a true example of international cooperation.)

This being the case, Jaspersen hastened down the corridor to the elevators and pushed the Down button.

In the elevator he found Nagashima, a Step Three in the Mediation Unit of Jaspersen's section. Bowing courteously, Nagashima returned Jaspersen's greeting; his perseverance with each syllable of Jaspersen's name made it sound like a phonetic exercise.

Striking a personal note, Jaspersen inquired, 'Your daughter at college now?'

'He's at the university, yes.'

'I thought –'

'Yes, yes. Just the one son.'

'What's he studying?'

'Humanities.' Nagashima nodded, smiling.

'Only the one play?' asked Jaspersen, who thought he had said 'Eumenides'.

Nagashima beamed. 'Yes. Yes.' The elevator stopped at the Organization Clinic and, with a polite farewell, Nagashima got out. The doors were closing when a peremptory voice cried 'Going down!' and the head of Jaspersen's department stepped in, breathing heavily.

'Going to the meeting, Olaf? I'm on my way there myself.' The Chief made a gesture of fanning himself with his own folder of Committee papers. 'My word, they keep this place hot. Wasn't that Nagashima who's just got off? I thought so. Hadn't seen him for a while – was beginning to think he'd got lost.' The Chief laughed benevolently.

'He was telling me about his daughter – turning into quite a classical scholar it seems.' They arrived at the ground floor and Jaspersen stood back to let the Chief precede him.

The Chief looked reflective as they walked along. 'That sort of thing, you know, Olaf, is the real work we do. Shaping the personal lives of our own people, right here in this building. Merging their cultures through their personal relationships; children adjusting to other environments, colleagues becoming personal friends.' They arrived at the top of an escalator leading to the basement. 'We hear a lot about the Two Cultures, but I say it's the Hundred Cultures we have to deal with. Bind them together, forge the common links –' The Chief paused at the top of the escalator to take in his vision of humanity manacled and trussed. 'Never did like these things. Fell on one as a child.'

Warmly – with a ray of hope, one might have thought – Jaspersen said, 'I'm sorry.'

'Oh – my own fault, of course. Didn't understand the principle. Step on and stay on.' The Chief did this, gripping the rail tightly.

'Understandable, though,' said Jaspersen, following.

'Hmm. Got to adapt oneself to the mechanism, Olaf, not fight it.' He was making it sound as if Jaspersen were the child who had stumbled. 'He who hesitates is lost.'

'It lacks', said Jaspersen, who as a student had read the German poets, 'the lovelier hesitation of the hand of man.'

'What does?'

'The machine.'

'Oh I quite agree.' The Chief took on a look of liking nothing better than the larger view. He added obscurely, 'The individual comes first.' He gave his full attention to stepping off the escalator before he continued. 'I want a word with you some time about next year's manning-table. We're getting overloaded in certain grades. Not enough slots to go round.'

Now they were walking along a wide corridor that sloped downwards, as it reached the Committee Room, like an undersea tunnel. Officials carrying papers came towards them and passed on purposefully, like salmon headed upstream. There was a multiplicity of doors, and a notice board that listed meetings. Another board displayed glossy photographs for the use of the press – the Spanish delegate enjoying a joke with the Custodian of Refugees, the Soviet representative opening the Children's Art Exhibit. When he reached a pair of handsome doors, Jaspersen grasped one of the inlaid handles that had been the gift of Finland and stood aside to let the Chief enter the chamber.

The ceiling of the Committee Room was earth-coloured, the carpet blue: it was as if the skies had fallen. The room was formed like a theatre, with a high public gallery. The action, so to speak, took place in the pit, where a more or less circular arrangement was created by an arc of tables – at which sat the representatives of various nations, all labelled, like plants in a public garden, with the exotic names of their countries. A certain bloc of seats was reserved for senior officials from the Organization itself, and it was in this section, in a leather chair, that Jaspersen seated himself, directly behind his Chief. The discussion had already begun, and Jaspersen, laying the folder of papers carefully on his knees, clipped over his ear the small electric interpreting device attached to the chair, his face assuming as he did so the grave and attentive expression of everyone else in the room.

Ismet concluded his draft memorandum with the word 'implementation' and gave it to Leslie for typing. He then got up from his desk and stood at the window. Resting his fingertips on the inner sill, he closed his eyes. When he opened them, a face was looking back at him from the glass.

This reflection gestured, mouthed, nodded, and, pushing up the window, climbed into the room. 'Gave me a turn, standing there like that,' it said reproachfully, helping Ismet to pick up the papers circulated by the rush of air. 'Wasn't expecting it.'

'Why should they clean the windows on a day like this?' Ismet asked.

The man clapped the last memorandum down on the desk with an irreverent hand. He shrugged his shoulder before readjusting the harness over it. 'Orders from above.' He jerked his head skyward. 'The way I see it – there's more chiefs than Indians round here.'

Ismet said reasonably, 'But that *is* the way you see it, isn't it? I mean, you only see the offices that have windows. The offices of the chiefs, so to speak.'

'Plenty of Indians in the dungeons, eh?' The window-cleaner laughed uproariously, making Ismet regret his rational explanation. 'I'm better off on the outside, if you ask me. Watch out for the bucket.' Ismet had almost knocked this over in pulling out his chair. His visitor swung the bucket up over one arm and made for the door.

Ismet said, 'I'm sorry I startled you.'

'Should be used to it by now. Plenty of you looking out when I come along.'

Setting his papers in order, Ismet heard the bucket loudly put down in Pastore's room next door. A moment later, Pastore was in the doorway.

'Nothing but interruptions all morning.'

'Exactly,' said Ismet.

'I need Leslie to take a message to Jaspersen in the Committee Room.'

'She's doing a memorandum for me.'

'This is urgent.'

'So is mine.'

'I've already asked her to go.'

Nothing, Ismet thought, makes a more fanatical official than a Latin. Organization is alien to their natures, but once they get the taste for it they take to it like drink. They claim to be impulsive, but they're the most bureaucratic of all, whatever they may say. 'Whatever you say,' he told Pastore.

'*The combination and interplay of such components*,' the speaker was saying, '*within deeply rooted conflicts* –'

Try as he would, Jaspersen could not take it in this morning. He pressed his hand to the device over his ear. He even glanced surreptitiously at the interpretation dial beside his chair, to make sure it was turned to the proper language.

'*– obstruct the evaluation process . . .*'

'Personal life,' the Chief had said; 'personal friend.' One's life, one's friends presumably could not be other than personal, yet the distinction had developed. I suppose this is my official life, Jaspersen said to himself, looking about the chamber. 'Official life' sounded like a posthumous document, some tedious work of commissioned biography with all the interesting incidents suppressed.

'*My government takes the view . . .*'

Everyone else was scribbling now, on scraps of paper, on the margins of documents, on pads provided for the purpose.

'*My government thinks, my government feels . . .*'

It gave him a sense of isolation, being the only one having personal thoughts in such an official chamber.

'*Bearing in mind my government's long devotion –*'

One said 'relationship' nowadays about those one loved, and put one's friends in slots: words like 'devotion' were reserved for official purposes.

A young man in grey had come to where Jaspersen sat, at the end of the row of seats, and was handing out copies of an amendment. Jaspersen, passing them along, thought how like church it all was. The deferential hush, the single voice intoning. O Organization, wherever two or three are gathered together in thy name. . . . Jaspersen gave an unholy laugh.

Someone sitting beside the Chairman looked round repressively. One or two acolytes – the man in grey, a woman in black – silently carried papers back and forth across the room. The man had the stubby, earnest walk of a schoolboy; the woman appeared to glide over the blue carpet. In a man, Jaspersen thought, one could always see the child; whereas in a little girl one could always foresee the woman. The child Jaspersen who long ago had laughed in church, laughed in the schoolroom, had no place here, not even in memory. The idea that these guarded Committee faces had ever been childlike, or that they were sometimes even now transfigured by secular passions, was totally irrelevant.

'*– to the preservation of freedom. For if freedom is to be effectively preserved, a solution must be found –*'

One would have thought freedom was a museum piece –

some extinct creature being pickled in a jar of spirits. The voice went on, on. Jaspersen's father, a gaunt old man who loved Schiller and had no knowledge of world affairs, would have quoted 'No incantation can compel the gods' (might even, for he was getting quite eccentric, have quoted it out loud), but Jaspersen knew better; had more than once thrown in his lot with incantations in this very room and seen the gods compelled. Was it not worth while, this compelling of the gods in a good cause? And if so, why could Jaspersen not rejoice as he sat there this morning? The trouble was, official life had grown so remote from life itself.

'– together with adequate safeguards . . .'

Jaspersen was not a man to succumb to despair: in fact, with his quick walk, he had quite outdistanced it. He would never ask himself 'What will become of me?' – much less the more terrible question 'What has become of me?' Here, however, twenty feet underground, in filtered air and fluorescent light, amid the aspirations ratified by one hundred member nations, a certain depression had managed – God knew how – to penetrate. There is no armour, there are no adequate safeguards. Deeply rooted conflicts are within us and obstruct the evaluation process.

Leslie sauntered down the corridor, her head uncharacteristically lowered as she studied the effect of her new shoes, which buttoned across the instep. When the elevator came, she got in jauntily. She liked to have errands away from the section, and often combined them with a leisurely coffee in the cafeteria or a visit to her friends in the filing room. Her sense of responsibility took her first to the main floor, where she got out. Descending to the basement, she stood on her toes to avoid wedging her vinyl heels in the grooves of the escalator. At the end of a corridor, a guard admitted her to the Committee Room, and she discovered Jaspersen sitting in a row of seats near the door.

A speech was being made, and Jaspersen was listening so intently that she could not attract his attention. Someone motioned her to sit down behind him and wait, and she did this, feeling important as she sank into the leather seat and watched her skirt draw back above her white knitted knees. The room was brightly, hotly lit, and was decorated – somewhat datedly, Leslie thought – in blond wood and blue furnishings. Absently folding the message for Jaspersen over and over until it began to part at the creases, Leslie looked curiously up at the half-empty public gallery and the glass booths of the interpreters. This was more like the real thing: more, in fact, like television. It was the setting in which Leslie had imagined herself when she applied to the Organization, and of which she had not, until now, caught a single glimpse. Her duties consisted in the main of inter-leaving pages with carbon-paper and typing on them at someone else's dictation. Yet Leslie had repeatedly been told by her superiors that what was wanted was someone who would take an interest in this work. What was wanted, Leslie concluded, was some kind of a nut.

Leslie did not care to know what was going on here in the Committee; since everyone else obviously did know, involvement on her part seemed unnecessary. She felt agreeably secure in the presence of all these diligent faces. And Jaspersen, she noticed, was the most engrossed of all, his elbow bent on his knee, his hand supporting his intent brow.

'*Recognizing the basic fluidity of the situation*' – the speaker paused, poured water into a glass – '*and in the firm conviction*' – he drank – '*that the pooling of resources . . .*'

When Jaspersen raised his head, a hand appeared at his elbow. It was a curious little hand, plump and pink with astonishing silver nails. Some of these nails were of oriental attenuation, others were bluntly broken off. Jaspersen, staring at the hand, was tempted to take it in his own. However, he merely accepted a pleated paper from its irregular talons.

He opened the paper, turned it round, and read. 'Unification is postponed.'

Jaspersen sat still for a moment or two, with the paper in his hand. He then put it in his folder and dismissed Leslie with a backward nod. He leant forward and touched his own hand to the elbow in front of him.

The Chief's head veered to a familiar attitude – not detached from the proceedings of the meeting, yet inclined, receptive, authoritative. It was an attitude of head and shoulders that had been perfected within the Organization and was best demonstrated on the floor of a large conference room.

Jaspersen whispered into the leaning ear. 'Unification is postponed.'

The ear appeared to frown. 'Not coming up?'

'Not today.'

'*– and fervently believing in the vital importance –*'

'Nothing to stay for then,' the Chief murmured, turning further round.

'*– and crucial significance –*'

'Nothing at all.'

They slid out of their seats furtively, like patrons leaving a bad film. Outside, Jaspersen said, 'Now we'll never know who did it.'

The Chief had a way of permitting a joke to register while denying it official recognition. 'I'm anxious', he said gravely, 'to have our item come up.'

The postponement of Unification had gone to Jaspersen's head. 'You realize', he said, 'that they may not approve of what we've done?'

The Chief smiled tolerantly. 'We must know how to accept criticism, Olaf.' He spoke as if it were some useless gift to be stowed in a closet as soon as the guests had gone. 'A most helpful discussion of Item Five, I thought, by the way.'

'Didn't quite get it,' Jaspersen said.

'Not get it?' The Chief had not known Jaspersen in this mood before. For a moment it seemed that he was going to stop in his tracks, half-way up the sloping corridor, on the rug donated by the Republic of Panama. 'Not get what?'

Jaspersen took hold of himself: he did not want to go too far. (To go too far, in the Organization, was to travel no great distance.) 'Oh – just an unfortunate phrase or two, perhaps –' They had reached the Up escalator, and the Chief had paused and was frowning. Pulling himself together at last, looking more like himself than he had done all morning, Jaspersen went on hurriedly, 'In an otherwise excellent speech.'

The Chief looked pleased, even relieved. Gripping the escalator rail, he stepped on and stayed on. So did Jaspersen, and they surfaced together at the high rise of the elevators, each tightly clasping his resolution.

Arriving back in his office, Jaspersen found his In-tray fuller than ever, his blotter studded with messages. The office was quiet. It was time for lunch – time for Subsidiary and Specialized to converge on cafeteria and dining-room; for cronies from Public Relations, from Logistics, from Finance or Personnel to take up their positions on the warm ingle-benches about the Disarmament Bar; time for Jaspersen to send out for his plain yoghurt and ripe banana. He sat down at his desk and began to go through the messages. Can you address the Assembly of Non-Accredited Groups next Monday? Human Dignity Section will call back. Please call Mr Kauer in Forceful Implementation of Peace Treaties. Long-Range Planning has been trying to reach you. This last slip was marked RUSH.

'You all right, Olaf?' Pastore inquired from the doorway.

Jaspersen lifted his head in a manner intended to keep

Pastore from entering. 'Everything go smoothly up here this morning?'

'Everything was as usual,' Pastore said evasively. 'Unification is now set for tomorrow.'

'I guessed as much.'

'You all right?' Pastore asked again, hesitantly setting foot on the carpet.

'Well – I was feeling a bit low this morning, as a matter of fact. Feel better now. It was probably the weather.'

'You know what it is.' Pastore nodded. 'I've been talking to Luba. She has an idea that Tuesdays are some sort of psychological low-point. It's an interesting theory – you talk to her about it. She thinks Tuesdays are the worst.'

7. A Sense of Mission

'Carry your bags, Miss?'

It was the first remark addressed to her by those she had come to serve.

'A taxi?'

She nodded, reluctant to begin by speaking English, startled to find her language apparent. She spoke to the porter slowly in Italian, the lingua franca of this island. Someone was to have met her; they hadn't come. Yes, she would go to the hotel. Which hotel? Well – what hotels were there? A Bristol, a Cecil? A Majestic, perhaps?

The porter smiled. What she wanted was the Hotel of the Roses.

Only hours since she had stepped into the plane from the winter night of a northern city, Miss Clelia Kingslake was breathing mild morning air by the Aegean. The sun streamed down on valley, rock and green hill, and the driver leant against his taxi in his shirtsleeves. Miss Kingslake's pang of ecstasy was not a bit the less for her having recently entered her fortieth year – quite the reverse, in fact. All the same, when her baggage was aboard and they drove off, she became distracted from her new surroundings, wondering if she could possibly have missed her as yet unknown colleagues. She was to have been met at the airport; so she had been assured before leaving Organization Headquarters the night before. There had been no one the least colleague-like in the waiting-room, and in any case they would have approached her. It didn't matter – she could manage for herself and they had more important things to do. For the time being, the entire region was dependent on their vigilance. After all, wasn't this an emergency mission?

The taxi rattled through a fertile valley towards the sea. When they reached the corniche, the driver slowed down, pointed out a row of Turkish houses, asked her why she had come to Rhodes.

She explained, on an assignment for the Organization.

'*Ah sì. La NATO.*'

Oh no, no. NATO was a military organization. Hers was a peace-keeping one.

The driver shrugged at this subtlety. He could not be bothered splitting hairs, and lost interest. Did she see those mountains across the sea? That was the coast of Turkey. And here, as they swung around a curve, was the city of Rhodes.

Clelia Kingslake had a glimpse of golden walls, of white shipping, of a tower, a fortress. She was revisited by ecstasy. A moment later she found herself in a driveway.

The hotel was formlessly vast, and brown – a dated wartime brown suggestive of inverted camouflage, as if it had been wilfully disguised as a military installation. Upstairs, however, unlatching the shutters of a charming, old-fashioned room, she looked down over terraces and a pebbled beach to the sea and, once more, out to the blue Turkish coast. The open French windows formed, with their outside railing, a narrow balcony. She pulled up a chair and, leaning her arm on the rail and her chin on her arm, sat there in the winter sunshine, happy.

Clelia Kingslake was happy because, first of all, she was a Canadian. Fished out of the Annual Reports Pool at Headquarters, where she held a superior clerical post, flown to Rhodes at one day's notice, arriving there to sunlight and sea, to trees in leaf, flowers in bloom, to the luxury of finding herself beside the Mediterranean – all this by itself might not have been thoroughly enjoyable to her strict northern soul had she not come to assist in a noble undertaking. She had been sent to serve the peoples of the Eastern Mediterranean in their hour of need, and it was this that sanctioned her almost sensual pleasure in her surroundings as she sat gazing out from the Hotel of the Roses.

She was, in however modest a degree, the instrument of a great cause: in this setting redolent of antiquity she even risked to herself the word 'handmaiden'. A dozen years earlier, in Toronto, she had diligently studied Italian in order to take her elderly mother to Rome. In the end, that summer, they had settled for Lake Louise, but she had kept up a little with the language. And this dormant ability had posted her now, miraculously, to an emergency mission newly established in the Mediterranean as an antidote to an international crisis.

An employee from the hotel was opening coloured umbrellas on the stony beach below. One or two hardy guests were bathing, although the sea looked neither calm nor warm. Apart from occasional shouts of '*Herrlich*!' from the swimmers, the only sound was the rhythmic crunching of waves up the pebbled shore. 'Sophocles long ago heard it on the Aegean,' quoted Miss Kingslake to herself, and the consummation of the familiar line in an actual experience, combined with fatigue from an overnight plane journey, brought a rush of tears to her eyes.

The telephone rang and she jumped up to answer. It was the concierge. Yes, he had put the call through to her office. No, no one wished to speak with her. However, there was a message: a Signor Grilli (the concierge permitted his voice a faint smile, for the name meant 'crickets') would come to see her at eight this evening.

She put the phone down. She had expected to be called to work at once and was disappointed. It was considerate of this Grilli, who was in charge of the new mission, to give her a day's grace, but she was anxious to take up her duties. She thought she would rest before unpacking and walking out to look at the town.

'Grilli. Downstairs.'

'I'll be right down.' She sat up, replaced the receiver, tried to think where she was. It was after eight. She sprang off the bed, pulled on her dress, combed her hair, alarming herself by muttering 'My God' as she fumbled with buttons and looked for her shoes.

When she came out of the elevator there was no one to be seen. The concierge directed her to one of the lounges. It was a large room beside the bar, decorated with graceful murals of the seasons, and the one person in it was paring his nails beneath the harvest. Miss Kingslake realized that, because of the name, she had been expecting a slight brittle figure, whereas the man who glanced in her direction, put away his nail file, and made a minimal effort to rise was a big man, a fat man, too young a man to be completely bald. His Sicilian ancestry – from which he had inherited the knowledge of the Italian language that had brought him on this mission – was not apparent.

She shook hands and sat down with an apology for keeping him waiting. 'It must be the journey.' She smiled. 'I was in a deep sleep.'

He glanced at her a second time, looked away. His hands quivered with the suppressed need to fidget. He said, 'You haven't come here to sleep.' When Miss Kingslake said nothing he went on, 'I've been here three weeks. The first week I didn't sleep at all. No time. Kept going on coffee and cigarettes. Just as well you weren't here then, if you need so much sleep.'

'I was assigned here only yesterday.'

'And if you don't work out, you're going back just as fast.'

The waiter came up. Grilli ordered fruit juice, Miss Kingslake a sherry. The drinks were put down, with a big dish of peanuts, and Miss Kingslake asked, 'When may I come to the office?'

'Tomorrow, Sunday. A car will pick you up here at seven a.m. I'll be in it.' The flat of his hand smashed down among the peanuts, a massive displacement that scattered them as far as Miss Kingslake's lap. He brought his fist back to his mouth and eventually continued. 'Give Noreen a day off. If nothing else. Noreen's been here from the beginning. Work! You ought to see that girl work. A truck horse. You know Noreen at Headquarters?'

'Perhaps by sight.'

'She's in our department there – Logistics. Not one of your fancy do-nothing departments. She's been in most of these emergencies – Suez, Lebanon, Cyprus, now here. If I had to go on another mission like this, I'd say give me Noreen.' Another peanut spun into Clelia Kingslake's lap. 'Rather than any six others.'

'Can you give me an idea of what I'm to do?'

'We all pull our weight here. I don't know what you do at Headquarters and I don't care. Here you'll do anything that comes to hand. Cables, letters, typing, accounts –'

'I can do any of those things.'

'You'll do all of them. You'll be in with the Cap.'

'The Cap.'

'Captain Moyers. He's been seconded from Near East Peace Preservation. Assigned to us as Military Observer, but he's turned his hand to everything during the crisis. A Canadian like yourself. But a great guy.' The eyes were wandering again, contentiously raking the walls, lingering suspiciously on Primavera. 'A rough diamond, but a great guy. He'll be here any minute. He went out to the airfield to meet Mr Rees.'

Miss Kingslake pondered. Rees was head of the Logistics Department at Headquarters. 'He's here?'

'Three-day tour of inspection. Oh, all the big brass have been through here this month – the Director-General himself came through, you know, on his way to the trouble spots. Mr Rees was too busy to come before.'

He pronounced it as if it were all one word, Mysteries. Miss Kingslake, her own gaze wandering, noted that the murals were by Afro. 'I don't want to keep you.' She allowed herself to add, 'I'm sure you need your sleep.'

Grilli was leaning forward, his hands splayed over the chair arms. All at once he changed colour. He hoisted himself up, vast and padded – it was as if the armchair had come to its feet – and shot out between the glass doors into the lobby.

Mysteries, surmised Clelia Kingslake, signing the bill. She followed. Grilli was bowed over a little cricket of a man, while a military figure strode about the lobby roaring orders in English. When Miss Kingslake came up, Grilli introduced her.

'Mysteries, this is Miss Kingslake, the newest member of the mission.'

Rees shook hands. He looked Miss Kingslake in the eyes and held her gaze. 'Miss Kingsley,' he said quietly, 'I want you to know that people like you are continually in our minds at Headquarters. Sometimes staff members in the field tend to feel forgotten. Believe me, they couldn't be more mistaken. I want you to know that it's fully appreciated, the wonderful work you are doing here.'

'Thank you.'

'Believe me.'

The three men were to dine together. Miss Kingslake was grateful that no suggestion was made that she should join them. While Grilli accompanied Rees up to his room, the Captain came over to Miss Kingslake, cap in hand, and introduced himself.

The Captain was also a fleshy man, though short. His

face was red and puffy. He wore heavy dark glasses with square dark frames. The regularity of his black moustache suggested an inept disguise – another case of bad camouflage.

'We're sharing an office, I think?' said Clelia Kingslake, when they had exchanged names.

'So that's his idea, is it?' The Captain shot her a necessarily dark look. 'More room in his office than in mine. What-have-you and so on. Could have requisitioned another office from the locals.'

Miss Kingslake said, with a helpful air of making light of things that was one of her more difficult characteristics, 'Oh well – it's an emergency mission.'

The Captain slapped his cap against his leg with annoyance. 'Emergency, bah. I've been in the Eastern Mediterranean five years. Seen nothing but a lot of so-called emergencies. Let them kill one another – best thing that could happen, what-have-you and so on. Or drop an atomic bomb on the lot of them.'

Miss Kingslake stared. 'The Organization –'

'Organization!' The red face inflated with facile rage. 'A lot of clots, that's what they are, this Organization of yours. A lot of clots.'

Miss Kingslake turned away. The Captain followed her to the elevator. 'And the Arabs. Don't talk to me about the Arabs.'

She made no attempt to. The elevator arrived.

'Vehicle at O seven hundred hours sharp. What-have-you and so on.'

Just before seven Clelia Kingslake came down to the hotel lobby. A second sleep, a bath, and a new day had made a difference to her spirits. Waking in the dark that morning she had thought the situation over. Was it not true, after all, that she – through no fault of her own – had come belatedly to a mission where others had been under strain? That she had encountered them, yesterday evening, at the end of a fatiguing day spent in the faithful performance of their duties? Miss Kingslake's heart brimmed with understanding as she climbed into her claw-footed bathtub.

How much she had to be thankful for, she exclaimed to herself as she climbed out. In all her time with the Organization, she had longed to go on such a mission. Not that she discounted for a moment her two years spent in the field with the Survey of West African Trust Territories, a rewarding experience in useful work and heartening *esprit de corps*: but SWATT, an economic mission, could hardly compare with a dynamic political mission such as this one. It was the immediacy that took Miss Kingslake's breath away.

Twice before she had been assigned to a peace-keeping mission, only to be forestalled at the moment of departure – once by a bloody revolution in the country of her destination, another time because of a slipped disc. Now it had all come to pass. Even a lag in the Reports workload had helped to facilitate her sudden departure: only two days before, she had completed proof-reading on appendices for the World Commodity Index.

Environment would always have been secondary to Miss Kingslake's wish to serve – adverse conditions, in fact, would merely have challenged her to make light of them in her helpful way. Almost guiltily, then, having fastened her skirt, did she cross to the windows and look out on the Anatolian sunrise as she buttoned her blouse. She had no right to expect that the fulfilment of her desires would take place in so much comfort.

She dwelt again, indulgently, on the encounter with her new colleagues. Grilli, a young man, evidently insecure, had been abruptly elevated to a position of unnerving responsibility. When Miss Kingslake's industry, her goodwill, made themselves apparent to him, his manner would change. And had he not himself described the Captain as a rough diamond? A display of diamantine qualities would soon put the Captain's opening remarks in perspective. *Pazienza*, thought Clelia Kingslake to herself, smiling in the glass as she put on the jacket of her best blue suit.

A black Chrysler was waiting in the hotel driveway, and Grilli was in it. Miss Kingslake greeted the Rhodian driver who handed her in, and asked his name.

'Mihalis,' he told her. 'Michele, Michel, Mike.'

Grilli said, 'The others are late too.'

'You aren't at this hotel?'

'Managed to find a modern place.' He jerked his head inland. 'Brand new. Air-conditioned. Music piped in.' They sat in silence. He looked steadily at the folds of her skirt, then reached out and took her sleeve between thumb and finger. 'Buy this out of your *per diem* advance?'

Pazienza, Miss Kingslake said to herself. She thought, This man is afraid of women. But she harboured the knowledge unwillingly and had not the faintest idea of what to do with it. The mere realization in itself suggested something unsporting, an abuse of power.

The driver opened the door. Rees appeared, carrying a camera and a brief-case. Grilli made an attempt to stand up inside the car.

'Sorry to keep you busy people waiting.' Rees settled himself on the other side of Clelia Kingslake. 'I overslept, I'm afraid. The plane journey, change of hours – it's quite an adjustment.'

'Certainly takes it out of you,' Grilli agreed sympathetically.

'I hardly remember where I was, this time yesterday. Malta, was it, or Herakleion?' Rees smiled benevolently at Miss Kingslake. 'How do you do.'

'Cecilia Kingslake,' Grilli said. 'She's the latest arrival. I think you –'

Rees shook hands, turning to her full face. 'Miss

Kingsland,' he said gravely, 'I know from experience that staff members in the field tend to feel forgotten. It's natural, being so far from Headquarters – natural, but mistaken. Believe me. You people, and the wonderful work you're doing, are in our thoughts at Headquarters every day. I want you to know how much you're appreciated and remembered.'

'I do know. Thank you.'

Grilli moved uneasily. His hands shifted back and forth over his knees. 'Here's the Cap.'

The Captain strode from the hotel, got into the front seat, turned and nodded curtly. Something had happened to him in the night. He was redder and flabbier, out of sorts and breath. The driver jumped in beside him, closed the door, reached for the starter.

'Well, get going, man!' cried the Captain impatiently.

The car rolled out of the hotel driveway. To their left, through a screen of eucalyptus leaves, they glimpsed an enclosure of long, leaning markers.

'A Turkish cemetery,' exclaimed Miss Kingslake, leaning forward.

The driver slowed down. 'It is the cemetery for civil servants.'

They passed through an agglomeration of Mussolini's architecture, and came within sight of the harbour and the ancient city. At this hour the walls of the Crusaders were tangerine, their splendid order pierced here and there by a gleaming tower or a minaret. Clelia Kingslake sensed, again unwillingly, that an expression of interest would not be welcome. Nevertheless she said, 'How marvellous.'

'A façade,' Grilli said, 'that's all this is, a façade. This place is poor as hell. Without the big powers to back them up, they'd be nothing.'

On the far side of Miss Kingslake, Rees beamed. 'I'd like a picture of this.'

'All right, man, you can stop here. *Momento*, what-have-you and so on. Not here, you fool, have a bit of sense, pull over to the wall.'

'If we pulled out of here, all this would fold up tomorrow.'

'The walls', said Miss Kingslake, 'are in some places seven centuries old.'

'Not getting out, Miss Kingsford?'

Having left the car, Grilli turned back, hung his fingers over the open window. 'Take my advice, girlie. Don't try to be a wise guy.'

Alone with the driver, Miss Kingslake asked, 'Where do you live, Mihalis?'

He pointed, 'Over there, on the façade.'

They followed the road Miss Kingslake had travelled the day before. Rees was to pay a courtesy call on the commandant of the airfield, whose name he read out several times from a slip of paper. Grilli would leave him there and return for him. (Later Miss Kingslake was to discover that Grilli, self-conscious about his inherited Palermitan accent, declined to deal with purer-spoken officials – a complication that had not been foreseen at Headquarters.) Grilli and Moyers spoke of invoices, of supplies and equipment; and Miss Kingslake, considerately leaning back to facilitate their discussion, was reassured by this talk of tonnage and manpower. Was it not all this, ultimately, that mattered on an emergency mission?

When the car drew up, Grilli escorted Rees into the airport. The Captain also got out and scrambled into the back seat, where he heavily and patriotically exhaled Canadian Club.

'That's it. What-have-you and so on.'

'What?'

'The office. The mission. HQ Rhodes. For what it's worth.'

Following the direction of his jabbing finger, Miss Kingslake discovered a large stuccoed cube alone in a rocky field.

'You mean, right here? At the airfield?'

'Converted military post. Lent to us by the locals. Supposed to be gratis, but they'll want their pound of flesh, just wait, what-have-you and so on.'

Some minutes had passed in silence before Miss Kingslake inquired conversationally, 'How far is it from here to Lindos?'

The door opened. 'You didn't come here for sightseeing.' Grilli climbed inside.

Having followed her companions up a short flight of steps, Miss Kingslake presently lost them in a maze of connecting rooms. The offices were high and wide, and floored with huge black and white tiles – hot weather rooms that were fringed with cold at this season. In the centre of each stood a new electric stove attached by its cord to some far-off outlet. These cords went rippling and wiggling beneath desks, under double doors, out into corridors; those that had not lasted the distance had been extended with others. The whole establishment was swarming, a nest of vipers.

Clelia Kingslake made herself known to the mission accountant, a Dane, and to the radio operator, a Pakistani. With a new, urgent perception, she saw that both were of crushable substance, and her heart sank though she said some cheerful words. A room containing the local recruits, boisterous with laughter when she opened the door, at once fell silent. Half a dozen messengers and drivers sat on the edges of tables speaking Greek, and on the single chair a little old man was fitting a roll of paper into an adding machine. She inquired for the Captain's office and they showed it to her, pointing out its particular black cord writhing down the hallway.

Following this, Miss Kingslake went to meet her Minotaur.

She found herself alone in the room, and sat down at what was apparently her desk, at the lightless end of the room. She uncovered the typewriter, unlocked the drawers. A sheet of instructions had been left on the blotter and was signed Noreen. Miss Kingslake switched on her desk lamp and began to read. 'Two pink flimsies Beirut, one white flimsy Addis–'

Mihalis came in with something in his hand.

'It's a light meter,' She took it from him and put it on the desk. 'I suppose it belongs to Rees.'

Mihalis lingered.

'Thanks. I'll see he gets it.' She picked up the list again. 'Headquarters all yellow flimsies.'

Mihalis leant forward. Miss Kingslake looked up.

'It takes one hour to Lindos.'

She smiled. 'Thank you, Mihalis.' With the best will in the world, she could not help feeling as if a code word had been slipped to her in prison.

The Captain's boots, having metal on them, were very loud on the tiled floor. 'What was the driver doing here?'

'He left this.'

'I'll take charge of that. Slack, that driver. Needs bracing up.'

'Really?'

'Like the rest of them. Go into that room of theirs down the corridor, they're acting up all day long. Good mind to report the lot of them, what-have-you and so on. Not the Europeans, of course, just the local staff.'

'The local staff *are* the Europeans.'

'Paid far too much of course.' The Captain was at that moment drawing an allowance from the Organization in addition to his Army pay. 'The way this outfit of yours throws money around. Not theirs, of course, so they feel free.'

Miss Kingslake lifted out the contents of her In-tray.

'Don't talk to me about drivers. Had a series of drivers in Kashmir, biggest lot of clots, what-have-you and so on. Rented a villa there, awkward driveway, narrow entrance between two concrete posts. Just room for the car, inch or two to spare. Made it a condition of keeping the drivers – they had to go through without slowing down. One scratch and they were washed up, through, no reference.' The Captain laughed and crashed his mailed feet delightedly on the tiles below his desk. 'They snivelled at first, of course, but they needed their jobs and they made it their business to learn.' He tipped his chair back, rummaged in the desk drawer for cigarettes. 'Don't talk to me about drivers.'

Clelia Kingslake was setting out the incoming cables, like cards for solitaire. She could see the concrete blocks looming, feel the sweat on her brow and on her hands gripping the wheel. And to think that only yesterday she had wept over Matthew Arnold.

The Captain spoke out on a variety of subjects, always exhorting her not to talk to him of these matters. He was unused, he divulged, to women in his office. He liked his own office, with at most a corporal in attendance. He was a man who lived among men. (Four years earlier, although he did not say this, he had abandoned a wife and child in Battleford, Saskatchewan.) He was accustomed to working with men throughout the day; to returning in the evening to B.O.Q.

This, though Miss Kingslake could not know it, was Bachelor Officers' Quarters.

'B.O.Q., that's the place for me.'

'I'm sure.'

When Rees looked in to retrieve his light meter, the Captain brushed away his thanks. 'Delighted to be of service, sir.'

'Sorry to disturb you busy people.'

The sun came round to the front of the building, and the

Captain went out and stood in it. He could be seen by Miss Kingslake from where she sat, planted with his back to the window and his feet wide apart. He had taken off his sun glasses for the first time.

Miss Kingslake got up from her desk and brought a mirror out from her handbag. Walking over to the light, she touched the discreet contours of her hair with an accustomed hand and took the opportunity to put on face-powder. When this was done, she held the mirror up and made a face into it. In a high voice, as if mimicking a child, she said '*Pazienza*.' After a moment she added, also out loud, 'What-have-you and so on.' Standing there in a square of sunlight, she rocked back and forth on her sensible heels.

She put the mirror away and came back to her desk. She made up a large number of cardboard files, feeling ashamed of herself.

Miss Kingslake sat in a chair by Grilli's desk, a notebook in her lap, while he spoke on the telephone. Grilli talked loudly in order not to be afraid, like a person in the dark. If he does a good job, she reasoned, why should I be concerned about his personality? She wished she were less exacting. She wished she were more –

'Outgoing.' Grilli dictated a cable, turning loose sheets on his blotter all the while. He drafted a short letter to his section at Headquarters. 'Date that today,' he said.

'Yes, of course.'

'I mean Sunday. Not "20th" – but "*Sunday* 20th", get it?'

He slapped down a handwritten list on the desk by Miss Kingslake's arm. 'Mr Rees is throwing a party for the government officials here. Invitations to go out today, champagne party at the hotel, Wednesday, six o'clock.'

Miss Kingslake placed the list on her knee, under her notebook. 'Any special wording?'

'Yeah.' Grilli read from the reverse of the paper on which Rees had written the commandant's name. 'To express heartfelt gratitude, profound appreciation for cooperation, etc., you fix it.'

'Shall I put "R.S.V.P."?'

'R.S.V.P.? Christ no. If they don't want to come and drink champagne they can go to hell.' His quivering hand passed unimpeded over the top of his head. 'What a day.'

'You've been busy?'

'Nothing to what it was before, of course.'

'Of course not.'

'The first couple of weeks. Just me, Noreen and the Cap. Kept going on coffee and cigarettes. The Cap's a great guy, don't you think? A rough diamond.'

'They don't make them like that any more.'

'Knows this region like the back of his hand. You should hear him. Not much of a talker, but when he gets going.'

Miss Kingslake said, 'He has a singular verbal tic.'

She could not tell whether she had said something unspeakable or merely incomprehensible. Grilli stared at her. 'I'm trying to get him recruited into the Organization. A senior post, of course. He's wasted in the Army. I've spoken to Mr Rees about it. The Organization, that's the place for him.'

Miss Kingslake said, 'He seems so at home in B.O.Q.'

Grilli returned to his papers. 'A lot to do. Been a big strain, this job. Not the work, even, but the responsibility.'

As long as he does his job. Miss Kingslake's pencil was at the ready.

'Being on your own, that's what gets you. Anything goes wrong, you're responsible.'

'That's what I imagine.' She lowered her pencil again.

'Dealing direct with the big brass. They want something – they want it now, like this.' He snapped his thumb and forefinger twice.

'Frightening, sometimes.'

'I can handle it.'

'Naturally.'

'Can't talk all day. I've got a job to do.' He tipped his chair back and locked his hands behind his head. He looked expansive – not only in the physical sense, for his face assumed a contented anticipatory smile. 'A letter. For today's pouch.'

Miss Kingslake poised her pencil.

'One flimsy.'

'Just one.' She made a note.

'White.' Grilli gazed upward, his eyes – half-closed in the act of composition – rotating over the motionless ceiling fan. His lips moved once or twice before he actually spoke.

'Dearest Mom,' he began.

8. The Separation of Dinah Delbanco

Cornelia Fromme said, 'The thing is, Dinah's got money now. Try one of these.'

'As if the Organization could care less.' Millicent Bass rolled her chair up closer to her desk. 'No thanks, I like the soft centres. Does anyone know how much it is?'

'Hard to formulate a valid idea. It can't be much, since her uncle lived to be ninety-four. And then, Dinah's ambivalent, you know. Says she'd like to go on working for the Organization, but that she's got to have this upgrading.'

'Think of Dinah making demands. I remember when she first came to Social and Anthropological. I remember when she could scarcely function within a given situation.'

'And now she wants a Step Two.'

'In the Specialized Category.' Millicent Bass went on, 'Of course, Dinah's a good person –'

'Oh, humanly speaking, Dinah's a good person.'

'– but very competitive.' Millicent opened the top drawer of her desk, handed one paper napkin to her friend and wiped her own fingers on another. 'There are tensions there. Plenty of staff members at the Subsidiary level are holding down Specialized jobs – there's no discrimination in her case. She's being highly subjective.' Miss Bass, a Step Four in the Specialized Category, appealed in the voice of reason. 'After all, are *we* properly graded, Cornelia, you and I, in terms of performance? We could all make demands if we chose to. Just one more, then.'

Millicent Bass, a large woman, belongs to a recognizable era in her profession. Her younger colleagues do not attire themselves, as Miss Bass does, in outmoded suits and golfing shoes. They no longer boast, as Miss Bass does, of caring for their complexions exclusively with soap and water. Their stockings are seamless, they have been known to dye their hair. They are, to use their own expression, changing their image. This metamorphosis not having as yet extended to their vocabulary, a conversation with one of them gives an impression less of change than of something having gone underground.

Cornelia Fromme had been Miss Bass's closest friend and colleague for eleven years, and should logically have been a slighter person. Instead, she too was a big woman with a penetrating voice. Nevertheless, she was the weaker of the two, and in that way the balance was preserved. Had she been of smaller stature, friction between the two ladies might have been less violent, Miss Bass being encouraged by her friend's stalwart appearance to treat her as a sparring partner of equal weight. Miss Bass made the most of a slender intellectual advantage over Miss Fromme; on the other hand, there had been a fiancé in Cornelia Fromme's past, and when driven to the wall she would appear with a small star-sapphire on her left hand. Their quarrels were famous and acrimonious, and always resolved in the same way: one or the other – but more often Cornelia – would come to the office even earlier than usual and leave a tastefully wrapped present on the blotter of the other. The presents were thoughtful – a chain with fastenings by which spectacles could be hung around the neck when not in use, a clear plastic rainhat disguised with clusters of white daisies, a rubber clothesline, complete with pegs, that could be fixed above a bathtub. The latest disagreement, a minor one, had resulted in the box of chocolates they were at that moment sharing.

During their temporary rifts, Miss Bass and Miss Fromme would circle the Section independently, each recounting the shortcomings of her friend. Newcomers to the office were sometimes misled into agreeing on these occasions, and even into adding their own parallel observations on the matter. All criticisms garnered by this means were subsequently exchanged by the two friends as part of their ritual of reconciliation.

'It's hard to understand Dinah's motivations. Obviously she won't resign, and she'll get herself marked as a troublemaker with Personnel. It's all so negative.'

'Of course she won't resign. Nobody resigns. Even supposing this inheritance paid her rent, she couldn't live off her separation pay. And what would she do with herself? She needs a group relationship, like the rest of us. She needs work she can identify with. Say what you like about the Organization, Cornelia, it's meaningful.'

'This is true.'

'It spoils us for work elsewhere, our involvement here with a realistic system of values.'

'And Dinah does work hard, of course.'

'That's just over-compensating. Compulsive.' Miss Bass shook her head. 'All right, I can't resist, but this is the last.'

'She says herself that she wants to go on with her work here.'

'That proves that this inheritance can't be much. No, Dinah's simply trying it out. When she adjusts to her new situation, we won't hear any more about it. All she'll have done is to defer her chances of a Subsidiary D. It's self-destructive.' Miss Bass lit a cigarette.

The two friends sat quietly for a moment. Then Miss Bass said, 'But Dinah's a good person.'

Miss Fromme nodded. 'A warm human being.'

'Yes, come in, Lidia.'

Lidia Korabetski shut the door and, since Gregory was still writing, sat down in the chair opposite his desk. Gregory was her chief. His desk was heaped with the spoils of chieftainship – a stack of memoranda for signature, each with file attached, a pile of flagged reports in manuscript, another pile of freshly mimeographed ones. These trophies at no place overlapped: Gregory was an orderly man.

'Sorry, had to get this out.' Gregory was a polite man. He pushed the routing slip he had written under a paper-clip on the front of a file and tossed the file into the Out-tray. 'Now look, I wanted to tell you – your friend did ask to see me, and I've just had a talk with her.'

Lidia put her hand on the grey curve of the desk edge. 'Thanks so much, I know how busy you are with the Governing Body. I wouldn't have suggested it if she weren't someone special.'

'Well of course, you're absolutely right – she's preposterously under-graded, and she could be doing better things in any case. Since she's worked on reports practically her whole twelve years in Social, she could be very useful to us here.'

'Exactly what I thought.'

'In fact, I'm going to raise it with the Director – no use my taking it up with Personnel at this point. She herself has an appointment to see someone there, but you can imagine how far that'll get her. Precisely nowhere. No, the thing would be for us to keep an eye on the manning-table. We'd have to have a slot for her – which we don't have at this moment – and *then* request transfer. But a good case could be made, and the main thing would be timing.'

'I'm so glad.'

Gregory lifted his hand. 'Just a moment. Not so simple. She doesn't see it this way. She says she'll only come here if she gets the grade of the job – in other words, a Specialized Two – as part of the transfer. Which is nonsense, of course.'

'Couldn't be done?'

Gregory clicked his tongue. 'Now Lidia, you know better than that. How's she going to get from a Subsidiary C to a Specialized Two in one jump? What we *can* do is to stick her in the post, then put her up for promotion at the next half-yearly Board, and so on.'

'What does it mean, "and so on"?'

'Well – first of all, she won't get through on the first round, so we'd put her up a second time, for the subsequent Board. That would be for a Subsidiary D. *Then* she'd be in a strong position to ask for the Specialized Two.'

'Several years, then?'

'Two or three.' Gregory shook his head. He was a just man. 'Not right, of course, but what can you do? If you work here, you have to go by the rules. Or you can always leave, naturally.'

'She's spoken of leaving.'

'She won't, you know.'

'What makes you think so?'

'One never does. Apart from anything else, what about pension? I'm not suggesting that your friend live an unsatisfactory life in order to collect a satisfactory pension –'

'An *un*satisfactory pension.'

'– but at her age one begins to think about the future.'

'That's what she's doing.'

'Oh Lidia, come on now, be realistic. What would her separation pay be, after only twelve years here? And in our society there just aren't that many jobs for women around – well, how old would she be?'

'She's thirty-six.'

'Say around forty, then. Not jobs interesting enough, that is, to make it worth while giving up one's security. You know that.'

Lidia said, 'I feel depressed.'

'Well don't be. I believe there's a way out that would satisfy everybody, and I've suggested it to her.'

'What's that, then?'

'Something that's been done before. I know of at least one other case, and I think an arrangement was made there about continuity of pension rights, if I'm not mistaken. It's this. She can resign from the Organization, and be re-recruited at the proper level. What counts against her, don't you see, is her twelve years in the Subsidiary Category. The Organization will know all about that, of course, but with qualifications like hers – and with our department asking for her – they'd probably close their eyes and pretend they'd never seen her before. They can be decent about things like that, you know. Much simpler to come in afresh as a Specialized staff member than to try to make the leap from a Subsidiary C.'

'You mean – her experience here doesn't help her?'

'I'm trying to tell you, Lidia, it counts *against* her – the fact of her having accepted the Subsidiary Category in the first place.' Gregory's eyes were wandering over his In-tray. 'Well, there's no guarantee, and she should look into it carefully before taking the plunge. But that's my advice, for what it's worth.'

'What did she say to this?'

'Oh, I think she may very well try it. She had me go over it all a second time, to make sure she'd got it straight. She said it was certainly something to think about. So let's see what she decides.'

Lidia got up. 'I won't take up more of your time. But thank you for seeing Dinah.'

'Not a bit. I'll be glad to help her when the time comes. If you knew the trouble we have getting competent people for this kind of work – really, it's to our advantage to grab her if we can.'

'Thanks anyway.'

'Oh there's no generosity involved. Leave the door open, if you would.'

Mr Clifford Glendenning was staring at a telegram when his colleague Mr Bekkus knocked and entered. It had been a busy morning for Glendenning, who was concerned with recruiting technicians from the corners of the earth to serve on short-term contracts in the Organization's aid programmes. Only yesterday, in consulting the roster of those who had already completed such assignments, he had hit on the perfect chap to work with chemicals in the Congo. A cable had gone out to Paris, and here was the reply. Clifford Glendenning was standing up, leaning on the desk with both palms and staring at it:

PAS ENCORE PAYÉ POUR LA MISSION PRÉCÉDENTE.

That was not all. There had been, in addition, in a single morning, a statistician who wanted to take his dog with him to Katmandu, an expert in basic hygiene who had sent his laundry home from Baghdad in the diplomatic pouch, and the discovery of an impostor in the port facilities team on the Persian Gulf. (This last was the worst, since the recipient government had recently commended him as the best expert ever assigned there.)

Bekkus made his appearance with a paper in his hand. He came in and stood across the desk from Glendenning. 'You once straightened me out on this Moslem nomenclature, Clifford, but I've lost track again. Too much on my mind. What name does an individual like this get filed under?'

Glendenning took the form held out by Bekkus, sat down, and studied it. 'An easy one,' he said, and smiled. Glendenning had a smile that turned up tightly at the corners and in this way matched his heavy eyebrows, which he had also trained into upward flourishes. The combination gave him a look of being between inverted commas. 'Proper name, Mohammad; Ali's his father's name; and Abdulkader was his grandfather.'

'What about this Hadji part?'

'That just means he's been to Mecca.'

'And what's Scek?'

'That means his father was a religious leader. I wouldn't worry about that.'

'Then what's this "Néant"? That's what I originally had him filed under.' Bekkus, seated now, leant across and pointed.

Glendenning looked hard. After a moment he said, 'Forget that. That's French for "nil". It's supposed to be in the box below, where it says *Marital Status*.'

Bekkus sighed. 'This Moslem nomenclature certainly presents administrative problems.'

'If you think so, Rudie, it's just as well you weren't with me at Quetta.' Glendenning had spent some part of his youth as an official in what is now Pakistan. 'Ten thousand people in my bailiwick there, and every last one of them had a name, I assure you.' Glendenning often spoke of these greater responsibilities of his past, oddly emphasizing his reduced authority, 'Ministers of human fate, we were, Rudie. Ministers of human fate.' When Bekkus looked blank, he added with a four-cornered smile, 'Thomas Gray. Ode on a Distant Prospect of Eton College.'

Bekkus objected. 'But yours was a multi-purpose, paternalistic administration.'

'It was.'

'You had built-in flexibility. You were operating within a broader framework.'

'We were.'

'It left room for scope.' Bekkus crossed one knee over the other. 'There was area for dialogue. Here at the Organization, on the other hand, we're functioning within unformulated personal situations, even at the decision-making level. Your post at least relates to staff members in the field, and involves less inter-facing. Whereas in my outfit we're continually evaluating the individual problems of Headquarters staff. And there's no more time-consuming subject-matter, I can tell you.' Bekkus shook his head. '*Per se*.'

'Oh don't I know.' Glendenning nodded. '*Per se.*'

'I wasted half an hour this morning trying to tell a staff member from Social and Anthropological Questions what she could easily have found out from reading the Staff Regulations. That Miss Delbanco who used to be in Conservation of Rural Communities and is now in Urban Welfare. A Subsidiary C, if you please, and wants a promotion to Specialized Two.'

Glendenning laughed. 'Talk about the Distant Prospect of Eton College.'

Bekkus succumbed to smiles. 'Well, I can't help laughing. But it isn't funny.'

'What did you tell her?'

'I told her, "My dear girl, *read* the Staff Regulations." Of course it's that old business of being in a post that's overgraded. Claims she's been doing the work for X number of years, why can't she have the grade. Exactly the opposite, obviously – the post was upgraded for reasons of geographical distribution, and only rates a Subsidiary C. If everyone got the grade of the post they were in, we'd have a nice situation, I must say. In any case, the Director-General's circular specifically specified that assignment to a Specialized post does *not* imply entitlement to the grade. Why don't they read what's put in front of them?'

'How did she react?'

'Oh – she's a conflicted little individual. When I notified her of non-entitlement she said – in a voice that was supposed to create some effect or other – that it was about what she'd expected.' Bekkus smiled again. 'You can imagine how far that got her. Precisely nowhere. I said – with a smile, you know – "You know, Miss Delbanco, that you can always leave the Organization."'

'How old is she?'

'Around forty. Maybe a bit more.'

'Well of course. There you are.'

Bekkus uncrossed his legs. 'Oh, it's all in the day's work, I suppose. We're here to do a job and this is how it gets done. But the time it utilizes is unbelievable. Unbelievable. He took his document back off the desk. 'Ah well, back to the salt mines. You think this should go under Mohammad, eh?'

'I do.'

'And just forget the Mecca-nized part?'

'And the Scek.'

'Thanks for your help, Clifford. I appreciate it.'

Glendenning raised his hand in farewell, and completed the gesture by taking a paper from the top of his tray. 'Any time.'

'Have a good day.'

The paper that Glendenning had taken up was a letter to the Organization from a private person. Like most such letters, it was addressed to the Director-General of the Organization by name. It was written by hand on lined paper, and asked for assistance in augmenting the education of the writer, a resident of a village on the upper reaches of the Limpopo River. Below the carefully formed signature, there appeared the word 'Help!'

Glendenning drew a heavy breath. Because he was associated with the aid programmes he received all manner of misdirected communications. How many times had he not instructed the Central Registry to send such letters – of which there were hundreds each week – direct to the appropriate officer in the Fellowship Division? Tearing a sheet from the block beside him, he drafted the routine response.

Dear Sir,

Your letter of 6 March addressed to the Director-General has been passed to me for reply. I regret to inform you that, in accordance with the legislation governing our existing aid programmes, applications for study grants cannot be considered by this Organization unless forwarded by the appropriate ministry of the government concerned.

Alternatively, may I direct your attention to the manual 'Paths to Learning', issued by the Research and Amplification of the Natural Sciences, Arts and Culture Commission, an agency affiliated with this Organization, which lists fellowships and scholarships available under numerous international programmes. A copy of the most recent edition of this manual (RANSAC 306/Ed.4) may be consulted in your local public library.

With good wishes for the fulfilment of your aspirations, I am

Yours sincerely,